Copyright © 2024 by Maren Moore/R. Holmes
All rights reserved.
No part of this book may be reproduced in any form or by any electronic or mechanical means, including information storage and retrieval systems, without written permission from the authors, except for the use of brief quotations in a book review.

This is a work of fiction. Names, characters, places, businesses, companies, organizations, locales, events and incidents either are the product of the authors' imagination or used fictitiously. Any resemblances to actual persons, living or dead, is unintentional and co-incidental. The authors do not have any control over and do not assume any responsibility for authors' or third-party websites or their content.

Art: Senny
Chelsea Kemp
Jess Lynn Draws
Editing: One Love Editing

The Christmas List is a 36,000 word novella packed full of spice and all the Christmas feelings to put you in the spirit this year!

This books is meant to make you feel like you're watching a beloved hallmark movie, but add in all the things we secretly wished for but never got!

Merry Christmas
XO Maren

A Strawberry Hollow Novella

playlist

Blue Christmas- Kelly Clarkson
The Christmas Song- Michael Buble
I'll Be Home For Christmas- Cam
Red Bandana- Noah Rinker
Snow Day- Caitlyn Smith
Believe- Cam
White Christmas- Roman Alexander
All I Want For Christmas Is You- Mariah Carey
Snowman- Sia
It's Beginning To Look a Lot Like Christmas- Alexander Thoma

To listen to the full playlist click here!

*For the girls who have been good **all year long**… you deserve a present in the form of Wyatt Owens. Welcome to Hallmark after Dark.*

XO Santa baby

Small town

Dad

ance

oic

Welcome to Strawberry Hollow

Josie

one

"Hey, Miss Josie, I heard my mommy tell my Aunt Daisy that my dad is always *horny*. Does that mean *he's* like a reindeer too? Cuz of their horns?" Arthur asks, blinking up at me innocently.

You would think that teaching at Strawberry Hollow Elementary for over four years now would somewhat prepare me for the things that come out of my sweet, little cherub-faced kindergarteners' mouths, but I'm honestly not sure that *anything* could.

In today's case, the bright red, blinking reindeer nose and velvet antlers that I currently have on while I teach the kids about my favorite holiday is the instigator.

It's true what they say… kids say the damnedest things.

And believe it or not, this might not even be the craziest one I've heard.

"Um, actually, sweetheart, they're not called horns. I

know they look similar, but these are called antlers. Reindeers have *antlers*," I say brightly as I reach up and point to the antler headband on my head. They're wrapped in multicolored Christmas lights with tiny little golden jingle bells affixed to the points.

My most festive seasonal headband because only the best for my babies.

Arthur's nose scrunches, his mouth pinching tight as he tries to wrap his little head around the difference between antlers and horns… and to figure out just what that has to do with his *dad*.

Finally, he shrugs, his curious blue gaze returning to the half-decorated reindeer coloring activity on his desk.

I exhale the pent-up breath I was holding.

Okay. Phew. Crisis… narrowly averted.

It's the day before Thanksgiving break, which some believe is much too early to begin celebrating Christmas, but I do have a reputation to uphold, especially at Strawberry Hollow Elementary.

During the holiday season, I wear my favorite festive outfits and plan as much Christmas fun into our daily curriculum as I can. I try to make every activity educational but also *fun* because they're still kids. Kids who are full of wonder and innocence and who still believe in magic. It's one of the reasons that I love my job so much. My brothers have always said that I was born to be a kindergarten teacher, and it might just be the only thing we can actually agree on.

The Christmas List

"I have something that I want to tell you all. But... it's a secret. Do you think that you could keep a big secret? It's pretty important," I whisper as I lean in closer to the sea of wide eyes staring back at me from their desks. They all nod eagerly, covering their mouths as a few silly giggles escape. "I'm counting on you, okay?"

Lifting my hand to cup around my mouth, I lean even closer and whisper, "People in Strawberry Hollow... well, they call me the *queen* of Christmas."

A dozen dramatic gasps echo around the classroom like I've just told them something revolutionarily groundbreaking, and I laugh softly.

"But... Miss Josie... that means you're like... *royalty*!" Lucy whispers in awe. Her bright green eyes shine, and an awe-filled smile takes over her face as she tugs on her long, strawberry blonde braids. "*Christmas* royalty."

She's a new student who just transferred midsemester into my class, and she reminds me so much of myself. She's bright and witty. Curious, compassionate, and kind to her classmates. But the thing that reminds me the most of myself is that she's a self-proclaimed Christmas fanatic.

The very first thing she told me when introducing herself a couple of days ago was that Christmas is her favorite holiday, and she loves to tell Christmas jokes. Now, every morning, she has a

3

new one to tell the moment she walks into the classroom.

Even though she's only been here for a couple days, we've already developed a connection because, honestly, she's the most adorable little girl ever, so it's hard not to be completely taken with her.

I don't have favorites.

I love all of my students equally, but without a doubt, there's just something special about Lucy.

"I think that's the best kind of royalty, don't you?" I say, my lips curving into a grin when she nods enthusiastically. "Ever since I was a little girl, I've always loved Christmas. Of course, because it's the best holiday there is. So I will gladly accept the title of Christmas Queen of Strawberry Hollow."

Twisting my fingertips in the soft fabric of my reindeer-printed skirt, I do a dramatic curtsey that makes another slew of giggles ring out around the room.

Which just may be my favorite sound ever.

"Okay, we only have a few more minutes until the bell rings, so everyone work on finishing your reindeer coloring sheets so we can hang those up around our classroom."

The sound of crayons and paper shuffling fills the room, along with excited murmurs as my students return to their activity, and I make my way around to each of their desks. I always try to offer positive encouragement as a way to nourish my little minds, so I spend a few moments with each student, complimenting their art.

When I finally make it to Lucy, I glance down at the coloring sheet on her desk and see that it's already completed, and she's begun to draw something in the blank margin of the paper.

Her light, strawberry blonde brows are hunched tight in concentration, the tip of her tongue peeking out at the corner of her lips as she focuses intently on the illustration.

I squat down in front of her desk and peer down at the drawing. "What are you working on, Luce?"

Bright green eyes raise to meet mine, paired with a sweet, lopsided grin that shows her missing front tooth.

Somehow, the toothless smile only adds to how adorable she is.

"Oh, this?" she mutters, glancing back down at the paper in her hand. "That's my dad. I drew him with a frown because he's kind of... grumpy sometimes. But he has a really big heart... kind of like the Grinch!"

"Well, you know what that means?" I ask, lifting a brow.

Lucy blinks up at me. "What?"

"That just means that he needs *extra* love when he's grumpy. That's when we should give the most love, to those who need it more than we do. And you know what? I think you have lots of love to give, Lucy."

She looks at me curiously for a moment, chewing on

the side of her lip, and then finally nods. "I think you're right, Miss Josie. Maybe my dad just needs someone *else* to love him too."

My shoulder dips as I stand. "Maybe so. Either way, I love this picture. You did a wonderful job."

"Thanks, Miss Josie!"

I leave her with a wink and head back to my desk, which is my own brand of organized chaos, and tidy it up while the kids finish their activity. Tomorrow is officially Thanksgiving break, and while I'm looking forward to sleeping in past six thirty, I have so much to do in my classroom that I'll probably end up back here, like I always do.

Not that I'm complaining.

One thing I learned very early on… being a teacher is never a nine-to-five job, and since I'm painfully single and have no kids of my own… it keeps me busy.

And I love it.

I spend most of my nights and weekends lesson planning, cutting out things for activities, and working on projects to display in the classroom. Anything I can to make my classroom a happy, *festive* place for my kids to be.

A few minutes later, the bell rings, and the kids spring from their seats, rushing over to their cubbies for backpacks.

"Okay, don't forget all of your things, everyone! And your carpool or bus tags," I singsong, grabbing a few pastel-colored tags off the hooks and handing them out. "Everyone, have a fun turkey day, and make sure you *gobble gobble* all of the yummy food for me."

A string of giggles greets my silly joke, and I grin, watching as they all file out into the hallway in a flurry of excitement.

Lucy's still packing up at her desk extremely slowly, which grabs my attention.

"Everything okay, Lucy?"

She nods, raking her tooth over her bottom lip. "My dad said he was going to pick me up today. He wanted to meet you since he couldn't the first day, but I don't think he's here yet…"

I'm looking forward to meeting her father, not only because I think it's important to have good communication with all my students' parents but because Lucy talks about him with just as much affection as she talks about Christmas.

I give her a reassuring smile as I walk over and help her put her pencil pouch into her backpack. "That's okay. That just means you can hang out in here with me for a b—"

A soft knock sounds against the classroom door, and Lucy's face lights up, a wide smile splitting her lips. "*Daddy!* You're here!"

When I turn to the doorway and my gaze lands on his face, it takes my brain a moment to catch up with what I'm seeing.

Because Lucy's Dad?

Is *Wyatt Owens*.

The very man who broke my heart eight years ago.

My first and *only* love.

The love that I've never gotten over.

And I am not at all prepared to see him for the first time since he left all those years ago. Or at least... my heart isn't. Of course I'd see him with my end-of-day hair a mess, light-up antlers, and a glitter reindeer skirt.

"*Josie?*" he whispers thickly. His deep, raspy voice has gone breathless in shock, sounding nothing like the boy I remember.

Nothing about him is like the boy I once knew. In his place is a tall, broad-shouldered, devastatingly handsome *man*. The kind of man that would make my heart race on a regular day, even without the fact that he's... Wyatt. *My* Wyatt.

Or at least he was once upon a time.

I swallow, inhaling a breath as I try to remain calm. "W-Wyatt."

He stares back, evident disbelief flickering in his whiskey eyes that I could never forget, even when I tried.

I've done my best over the last eight years to protect my heart after he broke it, which means that I haven't looked him up on social media or even asked his grandparents or his high school friends how he was when I saw them around town. I've done my best to pretend that he didn't exist at all.

When he left... I was devastated. I wondered so many times if you could actually die of a broken heart. It was the hardest thing I've ever experienced. I thought Wyatt and I would be together forever, and looking back, I realize I was just young and naïve.

God, is this really happening? Is Wyatt Owens actually standing in my classroom right now?

"You're... Lucy's teacher?" he asks, as if the answer isn't already obvious, heady surprise hanging heavily in his words. He holds my gaze as I walk closer until I'm standing in front of the doorway where they're standing.

Clearly, he's as taken aback as I am by this new development.

I nod as I roll my lips together. "I am. She's such a sweetheart. I really love having her in my class."

My gaze drops to the bright-faced little girl currently wrapped around his legs, her gaze bouncing between the two of us curiously. I give her a small smile, and her green eyes twinkle.

I didn't even know that Wyatt had a child, let alone a five-year-old, but now that he's standing here with Lucy, I can see the uncanny resemblance between them.

His dark blond hair is unruly, the locks mussed as if he's run his hands through it for most of the day. I can almost recall what it felt like to tangle my fingers in that hair, and my heart stutters in my chest.

He feels so familiar, my heart calling to his in a way that it once used to, but also completely different. I never knew it was possible to experience both feelings at once.

"You look—"

"It's go—"

Our sentences run together in a string of syllables when we both speak at once, and Wyatt laughs, low and gravelly in a way that shouldn't have my stomach fluttering the way that it is.

He's always had that effect on me, and I guess some things never change.

Lucy tugs at the bottom of his T-shirt, and he looks down at his daughter, giving me a moment to unabashedly drink him in.

My gaze drops to the large work boots on his feet, slightly caked with dried mud and grass, and slowly moves up to the tight, dark jeans that are molded over his thick thighs. Then, higher to the mud-stained burgundy T-shirt beneath a thick, khaki-colored Carhartt jacket. I take in his wide shoulders and the strong column of his throat, which is covered by a short beard that's slightly darker than the honey-colored hair on his head.

When I finally get to his eyes, I find them on me, the corner of his full lips curved into a lazy smirk.

Crap.

My face immediately heats, bleeding down my neck as I clear my throat and force my gaze to anywhere but where he's standing.

"It's good to see you, Josie. You look... amazing," he says quietly, and my gaze snaps to his. His dark, bourbon-colored eyes seem to burn into me, and I nod, plastering on a small smile. Even though my stomach feels as if it's doing Olympic somersaults inside of me.

"It's great to see you too. I-I... didn't know you were back in town."

His chin lifts in a slight nod. "Yeah. Papa fell a few weeks ago and broke his hip. Even before that, he'd been having trouble keeping up at the ranch lately, so decided it was time for me to move back home to help out. It worked out perfectly because there's nowhere I'd rather raise Luce than in Strawberry Hollow."

I nod. "That's good. I mean, that you're helping him out—obviously not that he broke his hip. Will your wife be coming by this week to meet me?"

I'm slightly fishing, yes, but genuinely curious now that I know Wyatt is Lucy's dad.

Lucy's nose scrunches, and she says, "Daddy doesn't have a wife. Wait, Daddy, *do* you have a wife?"

Wyatt chuckles. "No, bug."

Okay, well, that answers that.

Clearing my throat, trying to make this less unbearably awkward, I say, "Okay, well, um... if y'all need anything, please, let me know. You know Ma loves any reason to bake."

Lucy bounces on her toes, her princess light-up shoes blinking with the movement. "Oh, I love to bake too! My grams is gonna teach me how to make the best strawberry pie there is."

"Well, she *is* famous here for her strawberry pie, so I have no doubt she'll make the best teacher," I tell Lucy with a knowing grin before lifting my gaze back to Wyatt.

This time, he's the one staring, and he doesn't look the least bit fazed at being caught. His lips tug higher as he says, "Luce, we gotta go. Gramps is waiting for us. Josie… It was great to see you. I'm sure we'll run into each other again soon enough."

I nod, offering a quick wave, but Lucy untangles from her dad and rushes over to me, nearly knocking me over with the force of her hug. I laugh quietly as I wrap my arms around her small body and return the hug.

Then she pads back over to her dad, and together, they turn and leave. I'm stuck staring at the empty doorway, my heart pounding in my chest and my pulse still racing wildly.

Holy crap. Wyatt Owens is home… in Strawberry Hollow.

For good.

Wyatt

two

"Welcome to Strawberry Hollow's seventy-fifth annual Christmas tree lighting!"

Lucy is nearly vibrating with excitement in front of me, bouncing on the tips of her toes as she peers up at Mayor Davis, standing in the middle of the brightly lit gazebo wearing a red suit with a matching Santa hat.

The white columns of the gazebo are wrapped in thick, fresh strands of pine garland that have red and green twinkling lights entwined within them. Dozens of gold, red, and green ornaments are strung from the arch, seemingly suspended in midair, along with deep red bows and tinsel.

It's just one of the many Christmas-covered spots in town, and they've somehow managed to fit as much shit on it as they possibly could.

Everything about Christmas in Strawberry Hollow is

a… *production*. And if I had it my way, I'd skip all of it altogether.

But it makes my daughter happy, and she *deserves* happiness. So if that means that I've gotta attend every over-the-top festivity this damn town puts on to make her smile, I'll do it.

I'd do anything for Lucy.

That's the only reason that I'm standing in the middle of Town Square, freezing my balls off, watching the town literally plug in a damn Christmas tree when I've got a thousand things around the ranch that need to be done.

"Daddy, it's… it's *amazing*." Lucy's voice is a whispered reverence, the twinkling lights strung along the tree shining in her green eyes. Those eyes could get me to do just about anything, and most of the time, she knows exactly how to use them to her advantage. To stay up past her bedtime, to eat candy before dinner. To get me to build her a tree house in the backyard. To buy her a new dress even though she has more than she could ever possibly wear.

"*You're* amazing, Lucy bug," I respond as I gaze down at her. "You know, I was just thinking… it's going to be pretty hard to beat this tree with the one we're putting up at home."

She turns to me with a dramatic eye roll as her hand flies to her hip. "Daddy, a tree that big inside our cabin would not be practical."

A gruff chuckle vibrates from my chest. Getting a lecture from my daughter about what's *practical* sounds about right.

She's barely three feet tall and only five years old, but make no mistake, she's the boss. And she knows it.

"Oh! Daddy, look... there's Miss Josie!" Lucy exclaims, pointing a few feet in front of us into the crowd closer to the gazebo.

Josie Pearce.

It's been over a week, and I still haven't stopped thinking about her.

Imagine my surprise when I walked into Lucy's classroom and saw that her new teacher was the girl who would always be the one that got away, even if it was my own stupidity that let her go.

It felt like my heart fell out of my fucking chest seeing her standing there, gazing down at my daughter with the sweetest smile and eyes that I used to lose myself in.

Logically, I knew we would run into each other at some point. Strawberry Hollow's the definition of a small town. I just didn't expect to see her... yet. I thought I'd have more time to prepare.

I sure as hell never thought she'd somehow end up being my daughter's *teacher*. And of course, Lucy's obsessed with her new teacher, our past unbeknownst to her.

It's been years since I've seen Josie, but it did nothing to lessen the effect she's always had on me.

My gaze moves over Josie's small frame, the tight green sweater that's molded perfectly to her body, and the dark jeans that hug her heart-shaped ass. She's talking with someone, her fuzzy-gloved hand placed on his forearm. Suddenly, she throws her head back and laughs, and my heart squeezes inside my chest.

I miss that laugh. I missed *her*.

I just didn't realize how much until I saw her standing there without being able to touch her, kiss her, pull her to me the way that I used to.

I lost that right when I left Strawberry Hollow.

When I left *her*.

"Yeah, it is," I say. "I think the whole town's probably here, Lu."

She nods before lifting her eyes to mine. "Could we go say hello?" When I hesitate, she puts her fuzzy pink-gloved hands together in front of her and pleads, "Please, Daddy? I want to tell her that I love her sweater!"

It's not that I'm actively trying to… avoid Josie. I'm just trying to figure out how in the hell we're supposed to exist together in this town. It's not something we've had to do before without being a couple, and that was a long time ago. We were teenagers back then. Now, there's an awkward tension that I haven't quite yet figured out how to navigate.

Finally, I nod, heaving a heavy sigh. "Sure, bug, we can go say hi."

Lucy's eyes widen as her face lights up, and in a split second, she's bounding through the crowd in Josie's direction.

Shit.

I take off after her, my strides cut short by the crowd that's gathered in front of the gazebo. It was easy for Lucy to push through because she's so small, but I'm six foot three, and I'm having to shoulder my way through people, barely able to keep my eyes on her.

Her strawberry blonde pigtails bounce behind her, the bright red bows she insisted we tie at the bottoms catching the wind as she runs.

"Lucy." I blow out a slightly winded breath once I make it to her, staring down at her with a stern look. She knows not to take off where I can't see her. She's standing next to Josie now, her small hand tangled in hers as she looks up at me with wide, puppy dog eyes.

"Hi, Josie," I say.

Josie's red lips curve into a small smile, and she nods. "Hi, Wyatt."

Before I can tell her that it was Lucy who insisted on coming over, Mayor Davis taps the microphone before addressing the crowd. "I hope everyone is having a wonderful night. I am so pleased to be here, celebrating yet another holiday season here in Strawberry Hollow.

Now, it's time to announce our seventy-fifth-year Christmas List competition!"

Josie and Lucy look at each other, and Lucy's eyes are wide with excitement dancing in her irises.

"As you all know, this is one of our town's most favorite festivities, and this year, we have so many exciting, merry things planned. In case you don't know the history of the list, it started as a way to help cultivate holiday spirit here in Strawberry Hollow, a simple list of fun things our community could do in town to enjoy the season. But over the years, it has evolved into *so* much more. The activities help make our small town more beautiful and festive and give back to the community in so many ways. And of course, it's also evolved into a friendly competition. And this year, we have the best list yet!" He pauses when applause rings out in the crowd, chuckling at how excited they seem to be.

"Now, a few rules before we get started. Teams must be a minimum of three people to participate, with a maximum of seven. The goal of the competition is to complete all items on the list—in your most festive fashion!" The mayor smiles, lifting his hand and shaking it in the air, causing the bundle of jingle bells around his suit sleeve to sound. "For every item on the list that's completed, your team will be awarded a point. And you'll have additional chances to be awarded points whether your team has completed a task that's fit the theme and overall festiveness. That's right, we can't do anything halfway here in Strawberry Hollow."

The crowd laughs, and he continues. "Now, you can pick up your official competition document here at the town hall, which includes the Christmas List activities, and I guess I should announce what this year's prize will be as well?" He pauses for dramatic effect before laughing heartily into the microphone. "This year, the winning team will get to ride on Santa's sleigh float with none other than the big guy himself to bring Christmas to town in the annual parade!"

My daughter shrieks, bouncing up and down excitedly, clapping. She turns to me with the most serious expression I've ever seen her wear. "Daddy... we have to compete. Please, please, please. I *have* to ride with Santa!"

"Lucy, I—"

Mayor Davis continues. "Remember, one of the only rules of the competition is that you must have a *minimum* of three people to participate, and above all... have fun! We want Strawberry Hollow to be the most merry, festive place to spend the holidays, and it's up to our residents to make that happen. Merry Christmas, everyone!"

Soft tunes of Christmas music replace him as he steps off the stage, and Lucy turns to me once more. "I'll do anything, Daddy! Please. It would be the best Christmas gift in the whole, whole, *whole* world!"

Fucking hell.

"Bug, I'm not sure we could pull it off. Grams is busy helping Papa get around the house, and this competition sounds like a lot of work. We wouldn't even have enough people to participate and—"

She whips those puppy dog eyes up to Josie, cutting me off. "Miss Josie, could you be on our team? It would be so much fun, and I promise my dad won't be grumpy to you. I'll make sure of it. I promise."

My brow furrows. I'm not grumpy… Okay, I'm a little grumpy sometimes, but still.

Josie's warm brown eyes flick to mine as she pulls her plump, red-coated lip between her teeth. Shit, is she really considering this?

I shove my hands in the pockets of my jeans and swallow roughly.

"Oh please, Miss Josie! It would make me so happy. You're the *queen* of Christmas, remember? We couldn't lose if we had the queen. *Pleaseeeeeee.*" Lucy's sweet pleading is absolutely wearing down Josie's resolve, and I watch her shoulder dip. I get it because I live with the girl every day, and I'm still not immune to it.

"Well, my family usually participates, but with my brother's wedding this year, they decided not to, so… I guess I can? But I'm not sure if your dad is up for that?" she says, looking up at me through her thick, dark lashes, asking a silent question once more.

Heavy tension fills the air between us, overpowering

the chill. Her eyes hold mine intently as she shifts on her feet.

This is probably not a great idea, I know it, and I'm sure she does too, but she's so fucking beautiful that my brain seems to short-circuit, and any sense of self-preservation that I have leaves with it.

"I'm okay with it. I mean... if you are? I'm sure you're busy too, so please don't feel obliged," I say gruffly, shrugging. I have no doubt that I'm going to regret agreeing to this, but whatever makes Lucy happy.

And I'd be lying if I said I'm not partially agreeing to it so I can spend time with Josie. Even though I'm well aware that it's not a good idea.

Because honestly, my life's complicated right now. A happy one, but still.

I can think of more than one reason not to agree to this. I've got my hands full with running the ranch while Papa is down. Raising my daughter alone, trying to be a good father and teach her how to be a good, kind human while giving her the love and attention that she needs. Trying to figure out what I want my life to look like here, once again back home in Strawberry Hollow.

There are a hundred reasons why I *shouldn't* spend time with Josie Pearce, and yet every single one of them I've got an excuse for. I'd be lying to myself if I said I didn't want to spend time with her, and most of all, I just want to make Lucy happy.

"So… we're doing it? We're going to be a team?" Lucy asks.

Josie looks at me again, and after a beat of tense staring, she nods. I glance down to my daughter, my lip tugging into a grin, and agree. "Yeah, Luce, we can participate."

She jumps up and down, squealing and punching the air like she's already won the competition, causing both me and Josie to laugh as we watch her. Damn, I've missed that laugh.

Nerves churn heavily in my gut, but I push them down, instead drinking in my daughter's joy. I'll figure out the rest later, including the fact that I'm clearly *not* over Josie Pearce.

And I'm not sure how I thought I ever was.

All those old feelings have already begun to resurface, and I've barely even seen her. I don't know how the hell I'm going to pretend they're not there when we're forced to spend the next few weeks together.

Fuck.

'Tis the season.

Josie

three

It's been eight years since I've been to the Owens Ranch, and as I drive down the long, winding gravel driveway to the cabin where Wyatt and Lucy are staying, nerves swirl heavily in the pit of my stomach.

I never thought I'd be here again after Wyatt left. Truly, I never thought I'd see Wyatt again either.

I come to a stop in front of the small wooden cabin at the back of the property, surrounded by large oak trees, branches heavy with a blanket of fresh snow.

My fingers tighten around the steering wheel as I exhale a deep, stuttering breath, gathering my nerves and trying to quell the wild thrash of my heart.

This is nothing.

I can be around Wyatt without those old feelings getting in the way.

We're doing this for Lucy, and that's the only reason that he agreed to the competition in the first place. I also couldn't tell her no, not when she looked at me with those puppy dog eyes.

I turn the car off and grab my purse from the passenger seat, then reach for the door handle before I second-guess this entire thing and lose the little courage I've gathered.

Once I step out onto the thick, fluffy snow, I hear the front door of the cabin open, and then I see Lucy run out, wearing a pair of reindeer slippers and matching pale pink pajamas with Wyatt close on her heels, an exasperated expression shadowing his handsome face.

I bite back a grin.

I think it's entirely perfect that Wyatt ended up with a sweet, darling girl who constantly keeps him on his toes.

"Lucy, get back in here. It's freezing out," Wyatt calls, and Lucy skids to a stop on the front porch, huffing an annoyed sigh.

"Daddy, it's just right *here*! I have my shoes on," she retorts, a hand on her hip.

I wouldn't necessarily consider slippers as shoes, but I'm not getting between these two. Plus, it's *entirely* too much fun to witness this little bundle of energy sassing her dad.

Wyatt's brow lifts, and he jerks his head back toward the house wordlessly.

Another dramatic, drawn-out sigh, and she lifts a

hand in a quick wave to me, giving me a toothless grin. "Hi, Miss Josie! Bye, Miss Josie!"

She slips past her dad and disappears back inside the cabin, and I can't help but laugh.

Wyatt drags his large palm down his face and laughs too, shaking his head. "That girl. I swear, she's gonna give me gray hair one of these days."

I shrug with a grin. "Seems about right. If I remember correctly, you were the same way, Wyatt Owens. Your grams and papa had their hands full."

His smile widens, and a flurry of butterflies erupts in my stomach.

My heart still battles with this version of Wyatt. Older and more mature than the boy I once knew, time only making him impossibly more attractive.

Carefully, I walk up the snow-covered stairs to the cabin. Even with my boots that are made for the weather, the boards are slick and wet beneath the soles.

A large palm appears in front of me, and I lift my gaze to meet Wyatt's stormy amber eyes.

I hesitate, mostly in some small act of self-preservation because I don't trust myself when it comes to this man.

"Take my hand, Josie girl," he murmurs, the gravelly tone of his voice washing over me, causing goose bumps to erupt on my skin, even beneath my thick sweater and coat. That's the power Wyatt has over me—

a simple handful of words can cause such a visceral reaction.

I think I may have underestimated how difficult it would be working together in such close proximity.

After a rough swallow, I slowly slide my hand in his. It's warm, rough, and calloused, familiar in a way that makes my heart ache. He leads me up the porch, and once the threat of me falling is gone, he drops my hand and sweeps his arm out, gesturing me inside.

"Wow," I say as I step over the threshold, my gaze flicking over the inside of the cabin. "It looks amazing, Wyatt."

He chuckles from behind me, *much* closer than I realized, and I whip to face him. His shoulder dips as he reaches to help me out of my thick coat. "Been a while since we were last in here, huh?"

His face splits in a cocky smile, the unmistakable flare of heat flickering in his whiskey-colored eyes.

Realization rushes me when I think back to that time, my cheeks burning at the memory.

Oh God.

Flashes of that night flit through my head, the crackling fire… the soft wool blanket, and the deliciously wicked things he did with his tongue, wringing pleasure from my body until I was limp in his arms. The guest cabin on his family's ranch was always a place we snuck away to when we didn't want to be found.

Suddenly, his thumb brushes along my bottom lip, unlodging it from between my teeth.

"One of the best nights of my life," he murmurs as he gently finishes slipping my coat off my shoulders and hanging it behind him on the rack.

I try to push down the memory, even as I recall every scrape of his stubble, the feel of his rough palms as they ghosted along my heated flesh.

I toe off my wet boots and leave them next to the other shoes.

An array of his boots, pink tennis shoes with butterflies, and princess dress-up heels.

"Miss Josie!" Lucy exclaims, sliding along the hardwood and nearly colliding with me. "I'm so excited you're here! And you brought the list, right?"

I nod. "Of course." I lift the small folder in my hand and smirk. "We've got lots of planning to do if we're going to win this thing."

Her eyes twinkle with excitement as she nods. "Yes, and I already told Daddy that he's *got* to make us his famous hot chocolate. I think my best when I have hot chocolate." She taps her temple.

Wyatt laughs. "She does."

Goodness, could she be any cuter?

Her tiny fingers lace with mine, and she tugs me into the living room. There's a fire burning in the large fireplace, the flames crackling and popping as they flicker. The raw wood mantle is decorated with photos of Lucy and Wyatt, the love between the two of them so powerfully evident that it tugs on my heart. There's a handful of handmade decorations from his daughter next to the photos, handprints made into reindeer, small painted figurines, a homemade garland made of popcorn.

This little girl clearly has him completely wrapped around her little finger.

"Here, we can sit here!" Lucy says as she plops down onto a deep red pillow on the floor in front of the coffee table. "I already got crayons and colored pencils and construction paper from my art stuff."

My lip curves, and I nod, walking over to sink down beside her, putting my bag next to me. I love that she's so excited that she's carefully thought out and planned exactly what she thinks we would need.

"So, the first thing on the Christmas List this year is… the festival of trees. That's down at the town hall. Every team gets to decorate one of the trees that are around town. There's a ton. The city plants a few new ones every year, and by Christmastime, they are ready to be decorated. Oh, and next… building a celebrity snowman. We have to build a snowman based on our favorite celebrity. That's fun!" I waggle my eyebrows at Lucy, who giggles. "Wow, there's a ton of fun stuff on here."

I list the events off one by one, and with each one, Lucy gets more and more excited. She's full of energy, bouncing on her knees, hanging on to each word.

"How about you start brainstorming team names for us? You can draw your ideas in pictures." I say.

She nods. "Yes! I can come up with the best team name *ever*."

Grabbing the construction paper, and crayons, she immediately sets in to work, her brows drawn tight in concentration.

Wyatt watches from the doorway, leaning a broad shoulder against the doorframe, an unreadable expression on his face. "Josie, wanna help me with the hot chocolate?" he murmurs.

"Sure," I say with a small smile, rising to my feet and following after him. I absolutely do not let my gaze drop to the tight, faded Wranglers he's wearing and admire the way they hug his ass.

Definitely *not*.

I probably should've stayed put next to Lucy on the floor because being alone with him is likely not good for my heart or any other part of my body.

Especially when my mind keeps recalling in vivid fashion the nights we spent in front of that very fire as teenagers.

"You good, Jos? Your cheeks are flushed," Wyatt says as he pulls a set of green mugs out of the cabinet and sets them on the reclaimed wood counter.

"Yes, just a little… hot in here."

His lip tilts into a lazy grin. "I didn't get a chance to tell you the other day, but I just wanted to thank you for doing this for Lucy. She's had a rough time this year, and while she's excited to be in Strawberry Hollow with her grandparents, I know relocating around the holidays is hard on her. Seeing her this happy... it means a lot."

I nod. "Of course, Wyatt. It's nothing, truly. She's a wonderful kid, and she deserves a special first Strawberry Hollow Christmas. I'm happy that I could do it."

"It's everything to me, Josie." His voice is low as something flickers in his gaze. A wave of emotion settles in the base of my throat. Before I can respond, he continues. "This move wasn't expected, and I hated having to pull her from her school in the middle of the year, away from her friends, the familiarity of the only home she's ever known. But there wasn't a choice, and I've been so damn worried that she would hate it here. That she would resent me for moving us here, but she's blossomed so far, coming even more out of her shell, making new friends. I think you and your class have had a lot to do with that."

"I'm glad that my classroom is a happy place for her. That's all I ever want for my students. It makes me feel like I'm doing something right hearing that. God, when you walked into the classroom, Wyatt... I just, I couldn't believe it was *you*."

Wyatt nods, his throat bobbing as he holds my gaze. "I was surprised to see you too. When Lucy told me about Miss Josie, hell, I didn't even put two and two together. I've been too busy with the damn ranch, taking care of my grandparents, and trying to keep everything from piling up to pull my head out my ass."

I laugh, the sound echoing softly around the kitchen, and he smirks. "When did you decide to become a teacher?"

"My freshman year in college. I started tutoring outside of class to bring in extra money, and I realized how much I loved it and how much I did *not* love finance. I changed my major shortly after. I've always known how much I loved children, so the rest was a no-brainer."

We made so many plans together back then. Once upon a time, we lay in the middle of a field together on the ranch, an old blanket that Wyatt had in the back of his truck beneath us, talking about all of our hopes, our dreams, and what the future looked like. I remember how the only future I ever wanted included him.

Until it didn't.

The only bad memories I have with Wyatt Owens are the ones when he left. The ones where we couldn't make it work. Everything that we ever did before that, every moment we ever spent together as a couple, was full of so much happiness that I constantly felt like my heart would explode.

"I think it's a perfect fit for you, Jos. I'm glad you found something that you loved," he says sincerely, his gravelly voice breaking through my thoughts.

I nod, pasting on a smile as I pull out the barstool and slide into it, leaning against the high back. "Thank you." It feels strangely good to have his praise directed at me. "Um... what about you? What have you been up to for the last eight years?"

"Besides being a single dad?" he teases, arching a brow. "I'm a consultant for an oil company, so I can do my job virtually. It's the only reason I was able to come home to the ranch and help Papa out. I'm sure you heard about the injury..."

When he trails off, I nod.

It was impossible not to hear about what had happened during my freshman year of college. Wyatt was practically a celebrity in our small hometown, on a full-ride football scholarship to one of the best colleges in the country. He was destined to play professionally once he graduated. He was so good he had scouts coming to watch him play when he was still in high school.

But then he tore his rotator cuff his junior year of college, and his football career ended in the blink of an eye.

I was devastated for him because I knew that was his dream. And I'd even thought about reaching out, but I was young and still heartbroken and didn't think that my heart could handle it.

"Later that year, I found out Brianna, Lucy's birth mom, was pregnant, and everything changed. I no longer had football, and unexpectedly, I was going to be a father by the time I turned twenty-three. So, after healing from surgery, I put my head down and focused on school. I knew that I had to have a way to provide for my kid, and that's all that mattered."

I watch as he stirs the cocoa powder into the warm milk inside the mug, his long, thick fingers curled around the small spoon. It's comically tiny in his grip.

"Can I ask… where Lucy's mom is?" I ask quietly.

His gaze lifts to mine, and a beat passes. I'm about to apologize for prying when he clears his throat, nodding. "We were young. Still kids ourselves. Honestly, we barely knew each other. We never dated or anything, just hooked up a few times. She decided that she wasn't interested in being a mom. Signed over all her parental rights of Lucy over to me when she was just three months old and then went back to LA. She didn't want to be a part of Lucy's life."

A sinking, heavy feeling forms in my lower stomach at the thought of anyone walking away from that sweet, freckle-faced little girl who lights up a room. I truly can't even fathom her mother not wanting to even know her. It makes me want to pull her into my arms and hug her.

"Yeah, even after all these years, I can still read you like the back of my hand, Josie Girl," Wyatt murmurs softly, his voice taking on a familiar tone that nearly makes me ache. My heart is a traitorous thing lately. "Bri hasn't seen her since that day. Never even reached out or tried to contact her in any way."

"I'm sorry, Wyatt," I whisper thickly.

"Don't be. She's the happiest girl I know. Every day, she teaches me something new about myself, about life. Lucy's surrounded by people who love her enough for what she's missing. And to her? She's not missing anything. "

I blink up at Wyatt. "You've raised an amazing little girl, Wyatt. Truly. I've only been around her for a short while, but that's evident."

He opens his mouth to reply when there's a loud wail from the living room, followed by, "Dadddddyyyy!"

Dropping the spoon, he runs out of the kitchen, with me following so closely behind him that I nearly collide with him once we make it to the living room and he abruptly stops in front of his daughter.

Without pause, he drops down next to Lucy, who's clutching her index finger in her other hand, a tiny drop of blood beading at the tip.

Wyatt's eyes soften. "Oh, bug, what happened?"

Her chin wobbles as a tear slips down her cheeks, which are rosy pink from the fire. "I... I got a paper cut. It *hurts*, Daddy."

"I know, baby. Let's get you all fixed up, okay?" His tone is soft and soothing as he scoops her up into his arms, cuddling her tightly against his broad chest. Lucy sinks into the softness of his embrace, and he tightens his arms around her.

The entire time it takes to walk to the guest bathroom, I watch as he gently rocks his daughter, smoothing a large palm over her hair. It may just be a paper cut, something easily fixed with a Band-Aid, but he gives her the attention and care that she needs, never once complaining.

He carefully sets her on the counter, distracting her with a cheesy Christmas joke that makes her grin as he gently wipes away the tears on her cheeks and places the sweetest kiss to the tip of her nose. Tenderly, he wraps a heart Band-Aid around her finger, and at the very same time, I worry that the old bandages on my heart may be giving way.

If I thought that Wyatt was attractive before, it's a dimly lit candle to the inferno of attraction that burns seeing him with his daughter. Being an incredible father does nothing for my already thawing heart.

And I realize I might be in *serious* trouble.

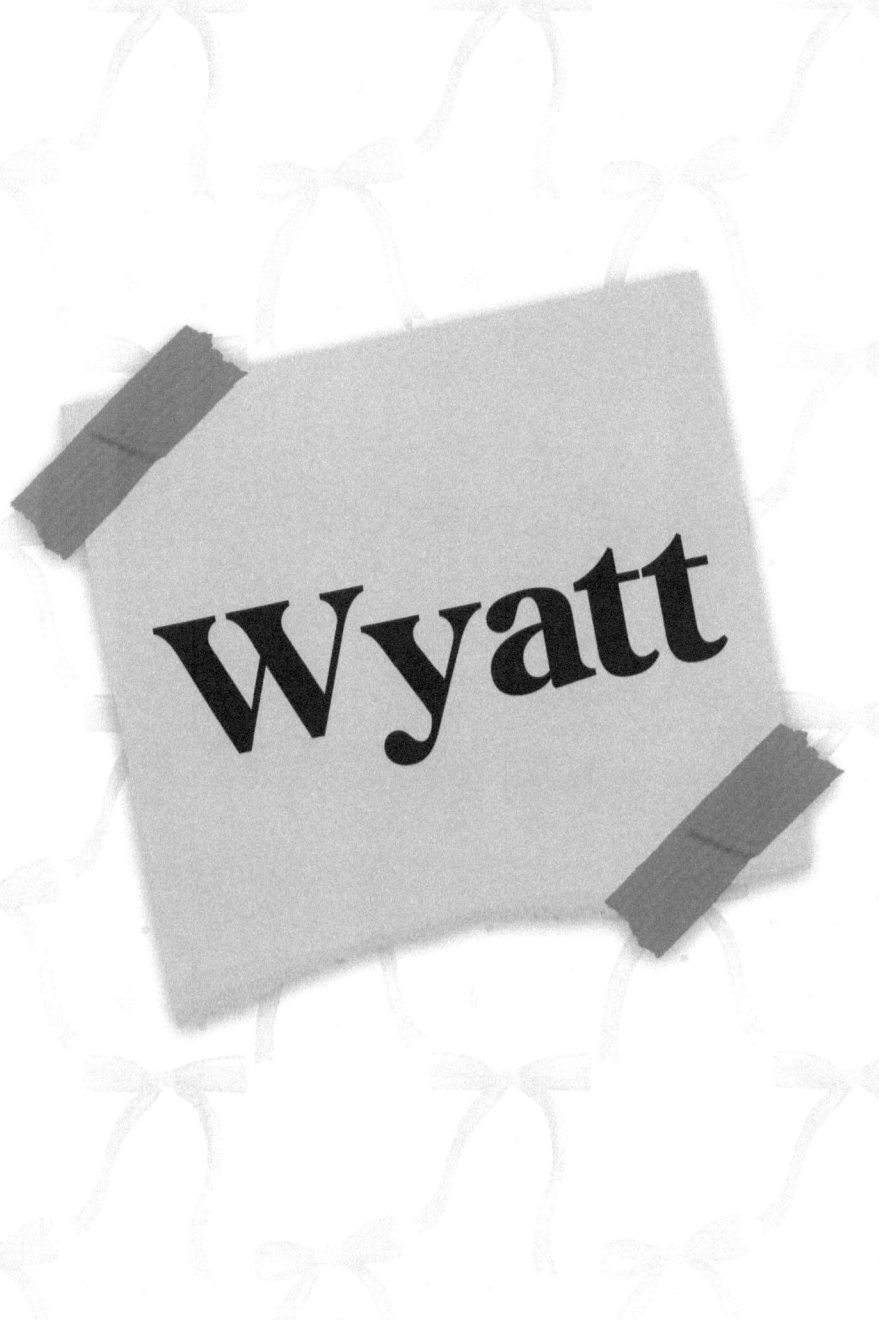

~~Festival of Trees~~ four

My five-year-old has an endless amount of energy. Combine that with her excitement for the holidays and being able to participate in the Christmas List competition?

Yeah, she's nearly got the zoomies as we walk into Town Square to meet Josie for the first task.

It took four bedtime stories and two hours before I could convince her to even close her eyes and sleep last night.

"Miss Josie!" Lucy cries, taking off straight for Josie, who's standing next to one of the large, undecorated trees in front of Town Hall. She looks tiny compared to the massive tree, which has to be over nine feet tall if I had to guess. Her long, dark hair curls from beneath the deep red pom-pom beanie she's wearing, the same shade painted onto her pillowy lips, which are split into a beaming smile that makes my chest ache.

The color makes her brown eyes seem like deep, dark pools of chocolate, and I find myself lost for a moment, her beauty nearly robbing me of air in my lungs.

With my hands shoved deep in the pockets of my jeans, I finally make it over to her and Lucy, and Josie lifts her gaze to mine, that blinding smile dimming almost indecipherably.

I have no doubt that she's just as affected by me as I am by her, and I'm not sure whether that's a good or bad thing… yet.

The few times we've been around each other, I've noticed the way her cheeks flush and how her breath hitches when I brush past her, her entire body going taut. Little things that someone else may not even notice, but at one time, Josie Pearce was the center of my world. At one point in time, I knew her better than anyone in the world. Years may have passed since we last saw each other, but that doesn't mean that I can't still read her. Even if we've both changed, there's still a part of me that will always be hers.

A familiarity that's like muscle memory.

And that's what makes it hard every single moment I'm in her presence. That and me wondering if a part of her is still also *mine*.

From what Lucy's told me, Josie has an affinity for quirky sweaters that my daughter calls "fun," and I see today's no different. It's a shimmery gold material with round ornaments dangling off the fabric. On anyone else, it might be silly, but it fits her.

And even covered in damn Christmas balls, my dick still twitches with the way it pulls tight across her supple chest.

Get it the hell together, Wyatt.

I watch as she bends next to Lu, removing the top off the container of garland and ornaments, and tells her to pick out her favorites before she stands and turns to me.

"Hi," she says quietly, a small smile playing at her dark red lips.

"Hi."

The air crackles between us, a heavy silence hanging for a moment before she clears her throat and shifts next to me, pulling her jacket tighter around her. "I think you're going to have to put her on your shoulders if we're going to put the topper on."

It takes me a second to even realize what she's referencing, her head jerking toward the tree, and I chuckle. "Yeah, probably so. She'd actually love that."

"Should we get to work, then? Not sure if you remember this about me, but I'm pretty competitive."

I nod. "Yeah. I remember. How could I forget anything about you, Josie Pearce?" Pausing, I hold her gaze. "Tell me where you need me and I'll get to work. We'll win this thing."

A shadow of something passes over her face, something I actually can't quite read, and she pulls her lip between her teeth as she whirls to face the empty tree.

Lucy's got the garland laid out neatly along the ground and is currently working her way through the box of wrapped ornaments. Josie squats down beside her, lifting one from the box.

"Are these... *your* ornaments?" Lucy asks, peering up at her curiously.

She nods. "They are. I've been collecting them for a very long time, so I have... a lot. These are my extra ones. Sometimes, I put up not just one tree at my house but *two*," Josie says dramatically.

My daughter's eyes widen comically, like she truly can't fathom having more than one Christmas tree. "Wow," she breathes with awe. "That's... so amazing! Daddy says that this year, I can maybe put a small tree in my room if I get all smiley faces at school."

I bite the corner of the inside of my lip to stop from smiling. I *did* say that in passing, but I shouldn't at all be surprised that she remembered it. Sometimes, Lucy feels so much older than her age, and honestly, sometimes, I feel like we've grown up together.

She's taught me how to be a father and a better man. How to be patient and understanding when I need to be. How to be firm and stand my ground when the time calls for it.

"I think *every* little girl deserves to have their very own Christmas tree," Josie says to her, reaching up and tapping her gently on the end of her rosy nose. "And I think I have some ornaments that you can borrow if you'd like?"

Watching the two of them interact like they've known each other much longer than the short time we've been in Strawberry Hollow causes a strange, tight sensation in my chest.

It's something I never in a million years anticipated happening, and now that I'm witnessing it... it feels entirely too good.

Too right.

I've never introduced my daughter to any woman I've been with. Mostly because there hasn't been anything other than casual nights since I became a dad, or honestly, really since Josie. After Lucy's mother gave her up, I vowed to myself that I'd never bring someone into Lucy's life who wasn't in it for the long haul. Protecting my daughter's heart is the most important thing to me, always.

Anyway, It's not like I've had much time to date because back in Sacramento, where it was just the two of us, even though I had a sitter I trusted, I much preferred to be at home with my daughter.

"You would... do that?" Lucy whispers quietly.

Josie never hesitates, just nods. "Of course. I know that you'll be very careful with them and take good care of them. I can tell you know how special ornaments are."

"I would. I promise!" Lucy pauses, glancing over at me, then back to Josie, and lowers her voice. "I'll have to convince my dad."

It's not quite the whisper she intended, and a low chuckle slips past my lips.

Josie laughs. "You do that, and let me know. For now, do you think you could hang these around the bottom?"

Lucy nods enthusiastically, grabbing as many as her hands can safely handle, and starts placing them around the lower branches of the trees. There's no rhyme or reason as to where she's placing them, but Josie lets her do her thing, never saying anything outside of encouragement.

After a few minutes, Josie comes to stand next to me, her gaze still fixed on Lucy. "You better let that sweet girl have a tree in her room, Wyatt Owens."

My mouth twitches. "Planned on it." I cross my arms over my chest, letting my gaze settle over her profile, taking in the corner of her soft, sensual mouth that's curved even when she's trying not to.

"Good."

I'm grinning like a damn fool, and I'm suddenly struck with the urge to press my lips to hers and kiss the shit out of her, despite the fact that we're in the middle of Town Hall.

And that she's not *mine* to kiss anymore.

But I never was great at following the rules, even back then.

"Imagine if they did this whole competition back when we were kids? It would have been pure chaos between us and your brothers."

Josie laughs. "Oh God, I'm pretty sure Jackson and Jensen would've gotten us disqualified before we even got to the second task. The whole point of the list is to make the town more festive, and you know the Pearce men mostly just bring destruction in their wake."

"How are they? Your brothers?" I ask. "Your parents?"

"They're good," she says lightly. "Jackson is married to Emma Worthington. Surprising yet unsurprising at the same time?"

Holy shit. I mean… those two have always had some kind of weird sexual tension going on, but I honestly thought they hated each other more than anything, so that is a bit shocking. Especially since Josie's family and the Worthingtons have always been at odds with each other.

My face must reveal that surprise because Josie laughs. "Yeah. Needless to say, there are no more feuding Christmas parties. We do them together now, so that's good. I really like her though. She's sweet and doesn't let him get away with anything. And his dogs totally love her more than him, which I tease him endlessly about."

I nod, laughing as I remember the lively Pearce sibling dynamic. "Jude? Jensen? Jameson?"

Yeah, all *J* names. Imagine trying to keep up with that while I was dating their little sister.

"Jude..." she says on an exhale. "Still the biggest playboy of Strawberry Hollow, flirts with anything that has two legs. Same old. Jensen... still painfully frank, endlessly sarcastic, and sometimes uptight. Jameson. Grumpy as always. Honestly, it feels like not that much has changed—same guys, just older now. Time flies by and stands still at the same time."

"Yeah, I get what you mean. Do you still collect your ornaments?" I ask.

She nods, rolling her lips together as her gaze travels to mine. "I do. Can't break a tradition after this long. I... still have ours. I couldn't part with it, even after you left."

That one small admission plants a tiny seed of hope somewhere inside of me. Whether she's ready to admit it or not, the fact that she couldn't get rid of it? Yeah, it means something.

"I'm sorry, Josie. That I left how I did. I should've reached out after. I just thought it would be easier for you if there was a clean break. Hell, there were so many times where I missed you so fucking bad that I almost broke, but I didn't want to hurt you any more than I already had. I was a stupid kid, chasing a dream that was always bigger than I was."

Emotion flickers in her eyes as her throat bobs with a rough swallow. "It... was probably better that way. I didn't think so at the time, but it would've been harder. Holding on to you after you'd already gone."

The words slice through me, and I hold back a wince. I hate that I hurt her, that I didn't even attempt to try the long-distance thing. I was so focused on my own goals that I didn't think about how she'd fit into the bigger picture. I truly thought it would be better to end our relationship since she was still in high school and I was thousands of miles away. But if I hadn't, then I wouldn't have Lucy right now, and out of all the mistakes I made as a kid, she's not one of them.

Letting Josie go always was though.

"I always thought about what would've happened if I didn't. Leave, I mean," I say finally after a beat of silence that hums through the air like a charged electric current, "Sometimes I regretted it, but Jos, it gave me my girl."

Josie blinks, her expression soft and sweet, like the girl I fell in love with all those years ago. "I know, Wyatt. I'm not angry or upset about the past. I understood why you did. You had the opportunity of a lifetime, and you couldn't pass that up. You had the entire world at your fingertips, and I never blamed you for leaving. It didn't make it hurt any less or break my heart any less, but I understood. And now..." She trails off, her gaze sliding to Lucy, who's dancing around in excitement as she places the ornaments on the tree, her pigtails bouncing with each move. "You have the most darling little girl, who clearly has you wrapped around her finger. She's incredible and has all the best parts of you."

"I'd like to think so too." I want to reach for Josie, but I stuff my hands in the pockets of my jeans instead.

"I just... Now that you're back in Strawberry Hollow, I hope that we can put it behind us and maybe even be friends?"

I don't immediately respond because I'm tossing the word around in my head, trying to make sense of what it would even really mean for us. Sure... I could be friends with Josie. But it's not going to stop me from wanting more.

"I want to be friends with you, Josie. But the truth is? I'm not sure if I can *only* be that."

Her mouth falls open, making the perfect red O, and I bite back a smirk. Before she even has a chance to respond, Lucy calls out, "Daddy! I need your help because even on my tippy-toes, I'm not tall enough!"

Chuckling, I reach out and use my finger to close Josie's mouth, dipping my head to her ear. "Do with that what you will, *honey*."

I use the pet name I know that she used to love so much, and when I pull back, her cheeks are stained pink, her dark red lips still parted as a stuttering breath escapes. Tossing her a wink, I walk over to Lucy and swoop her into my arms, ticking her belly until her giggles fill the air around us.

I know it might be crazy, that I'm pushing too fast or that it might have been the wrong thing to say after we just brought up our past, but I made the mistake of walking away from Josie once, and I'm not sure I'm willing to make the same mistake twice.

Josie

~~Celebrity Snowman~~ five

It's been two days since Wyatt told me that he wasn't sure if we could *only* be friends during our first task of the competition.

Two full days of me trying not to overthink every single word of that conversation and... failing.

Horribly.

How could I not replay what he said when, for so long, it was all I wanted?

There were nights back then, even though we were young and still naive to the real world around us, that I would've done anything to have him back. To change the story that had inevitably been written for us.

But now?

I'm an adult who's had my heart broken, who's experienced all the hurt that the world has to offer.

I'm not bitter or angry or resentful toward him. I didn't lie when I told him that I don't blame him for leaving to go to California or for ending the relationship. I never once held it against him for making that choice for his future. That would've been selfish.

But losing Wyatt was a hurt that I'm not sure I could survive again.

The sound of gravel and snow crunching beneath tires pulls me from my thoughts, and I blow out an exhale as I stride over to the front door just as I hear the low rumble of the engine cutting.

I swing the door open, pasting on a bright smile when I see Lucy, full of energy, bounding toward me. Today, her long curls are woven into french braids, the ends fastened with tiny little Santa hats that jingle every time she steps.

"Good morning!" she says cheerfully, holding up a paper bag of donuts. "Daddy and I got these for you."

I have a sneaking suspicion that if I opened that bag, there would be chocolate donuts with sprinkles on them.

My gaze lifts to Wyatt, who's wearing a lazy, knowing grin on his handsome face. He winks at me, lifting his shoulder in a shrug.

God, this man. He knows exactly what he's doing. Of course he'd pick up my favorite donuts, not even questioning that maybe in the last eight years, I picked a new favorite.

"Thank you," I say, dragging a look over both of them, "Come in."

Lucy breezes past me into my cottage, and when Wyatt steps past me, his tall, unyielding body brushing mine, a shiver racks my spine.

I wish that I didn't have such a visible, visceral reaction to him. But it isn't up to me.

My body seems to react on its own, traitorous accord.

"Hi, Jos," he rasps when his heavy boot thuds against the candy cane mat inside my front door.

"Wyatt."

I shut the door behind us, exhaling a shaky breath before turning toward them.

"Gosh, Miss Josie, you have the best house in the whole world. It's like the North Pole!" Lucy exclaims as she brushes a finger over one of the shiny nutcrackers on my end tables.

Honestly, that's the best compliment I could get. I mean, there *is* a reason why I'm the queen of Christmas in Strawberry Hollow, and it's not just because of dress-up days and early celebrations in class.

I am a little… extra when it comes to decorating, but I am a very firm believer in doing what makes you happy and whatever brings you joy.

And Christmas brings me immense joy.

So… I go all out and decorate almost every surface of my house.

Wyatt chuckles as he strokes a hand over his jaw,

watching his daughter flit all over my living room, trying to take in everything all at once.

"Queen of Christmas, huh?" he finally says, lips curling in a smirk.

I shrug. "There are much worse things to be in this town. Plus, the kids love it."

He nods, his eyes lingering on mine for a moment too long, making my heart pick up in my chest, and my pulse begins to pound. How does he so effortlessly unnerve me with only a look?

It's entirely unfair.

I cross my arms over my chest and tear my gaze away, walking over to Lucy. "Do you want to meet someone?"

"Yes!" Her head bobs in an enthusiastic nod as she sets down one of the gingerbread figurines back into the gingerbread village. "But... who?"

"Well, he's the most important person in my life outside of my parents and brothers. He's really special." I lift a brow, biting back a grin when I see a look of something like jealousy spreading over Wyatt's face.

I leave them both in the living room and walk to my bedroom, retrieving said special guy, with a slight spring in my step that I will not be admitting has anything to do with Wyatt.

"Oh my gosh... He's so *fluffy*!" Lucy squeals, immediately reaching for my mischievous, chubby cat. "What's his name?"

I pass him over into her arms, where he goes willingly, all too eager to have attention from anyone who will give it to him. He purrs, rubbing his fluffy head into the palm of her hand, making her giggle.

"Rudy," I murmur. "Wanna know why I named him that?"

When she nods, I say, "Because of his nose, right here." I gently tap my finger along the reddish, brown color. "He's a bit like Rudolph, don't ya think? Red nose and all."

"Ohhhh, yes! That's the perfect name."

Laughing, I look over at Wyatt, who's watching the two of us. My stomach flips when the warmth of his gaze settles over me, a flush beginning to move from my cheeks down to the neckline of my sweater. "Rudy is a naughty boy. He likes to get into presents when he's not supposed to. I have to put fake ones underneath the tree so he doesn't ruin the real ones."

"Oh no, Rudy," she whispers, staring down at him in disappointment. "Naughty boys get *coal* in their stockings. Grams said so."

I have to cover my mouth in an attempt not to laugh. It's as equally cute as it is hilarious, and I hear a low, gruff chuckle vibrating out of Wyatt. Rudy, on the other hand, is characteristically unperturbed by her warning.

"Lu, we're gonna be late if we don't get going. We've got a snowman to build, remember?"

She nods, giving one more tight hug to Rudy, then

bends and sets him on his feet, where he plops down lazily.

Once arriving at Town Square, it's packed with excited towngoers. Thankfully, the weather couldn't be any more perfect for today's task. The snow beneath our boots is thick, soft, and fluffy from last night's storm.

Winters in Strawberry Hollow aren't for the faint of heart. We always have heavy snowfall, and there are some days when I can't even get to school because the roads are so bad, and the plows can't make it up that high on the mountain until it lets up.

"Alright, ladies, what kind of snowman are we making today?" Wyatt asks, his brow lifted in question.

Lucy and I both look at each other, and her shoulder dips in a shrug.

I honestly haven't thought about much of anything outside the conversation with Wyatt at his house the other night.

"What about... Dolly Parton?" I throw in. She's another beloved Christmas queen, so she's the first name that pops into my head.

Wyatt tosses his head back and laughs. "Seriously, Jos? Are you trying to make a... *Snowlene*?"

Even as I'm rolling my eyes and attempting a scowl, I can't help but laugh. "Okay, I didn't even think of that, but that actually fits perfectly."

Lucy offers another shrug. I don't think she's as

interested as much in the who but more in the actual building part.

"Is this your first snowman?" I ask.

"Yeah." She bends and scoops up a handful of snow into her gloved palm, then attempts to fashion it into a small ball. "It didn't ever snow in Sacramento."

There's a warm feeling spreading beneath my breastbone, knowing that I'm getting to help Lucy experience some of the best holiday experiences for the first time.

Though it hasn't been long since I've known her, I already care about her immensely, and even more so now that I know she's Wyatt's daughter. It seemed like there was this unspoken connection that I couldn't quite understand when I first met her, but now it makes sense. She's an extension of someone who I loved with every ounce of my being.

"Well, we're going to have to make this the best Snowlene to ever exist, then, huh?" I say as I reach for the small tote bag of supplies I packed earlier this morning.

I'm prepared if nothing else, and I can't show up to a Christmas competition as the *queen* and not be wholly ready for today's task...

Lucy's grin is infectious as she nods. "Yes! We'll put my daddy to work, Miss Josie, c'mon."

I laugh, gaze moving to Wyatt, admiring the tilt to his sensual mouth.

God, he looks like a sexy lumberjack mixed with a ranch... hand? Or *something.*

I honestly don't even know the right way to describe him. He's a mixture of conundrums, but it's ridiculous how incredible he looks wearing nothing but a pair of worn, faded Wranglers, a flannel shirt, and a pair of old work boots.

He's deliciously rugged and still refined.

My eyes linger on his broad shoulders as he starts working on the base, the thick muscles of his biceps flexing as he packs the snow together.

I'm a little worried about just how turned on I am watching a man make a snowman.

Snowlene, I mean.

"You going to stand there, or are you going to help us, woman?" he teases, shooting me a wink while his brow lifts.

I spring into action, stuttering slightly. "Y-yes. Sorry. Okay, uh, I can work on the... hair?"

Crap. I did not bring... hair for a snowman. Pretty sure even if I did, well, it wouldn't be nearly enough to make it as high as Dolly's iconic blonde hair.

Oh! I have ribbon.

When I pull it out of the bag, Wyatt chuckles, shaking his head. "Ah. Good thinking, Jos."

Just as Mayor Davis announces the five-minute warning, we're putting the finishing touches on our Snowlene, and I have to admit that she's pretty incredible for something we threw together in just under an hour with not a ton of options.

Even Lucy, who I'm pretty sure has absolutely no idea who Dolly Parton even is, is impressed.

She blinks up at the snowman, her toothless grin spread wide. Wyatt squats down beside her and loops his arm over her small shoulder. "Now, that's a snow-woman, bug."

"Daddy! It's Snowlene!" She giggles.

"Oh yes, sorry, sorry."

I laugh before pulling my lip between my teeth. Wyatt rises to his feet and directs his attention to picking up the leftover supplies, and I drop my gaze to my feet when it lands on the tight globes of his butt in those stupid Wranglers.

Instead, I watch Lucy as she makes little snowballs and places them all around Snowlene, and that's when I decide that I'm going to make a snowball of my own.

One that I'm aiming straight for Wyatt's *stupid* Wrangler butt.

I bend, scooping up a big handful of snow and quietly packing it into a tight ball. "Hey, Wyatt?"

He turns, his gold-flecked eyes widening when they drop to the snowball in my hand and then back to the shit-eating grin on my face.

"Josie Pearce, you know better than to start a war you have no intention of finishing." My brow arches, and he shakes his head, holding up his hands as if I'm a feral animal that he's attempting to corral into a cage. Mmmm. This is going to be satisfying, I have no doubt.

"Don't you throw that at me, Josie."

Oh, I'm throwing it.

He's the one that should know better.

I raise my hand, biting back my smirk as he winces. "Josie." His tone is full of warning. When that doesn't work, he says, "Now, hon—"

Smack.

The snowball hits him directly in the center of his forehead, coating almost his entire face, pieces clinging to his beard and dusting along the front of his flannel. His mouth hangs open as if he can't actually believe I threw it at him.

"Daddy, Miss Josie got you *in the face!*" Lucy cackles, nearly collapsing to the ground from how hard she's laughing. "Do it again!"

Wyatt wants to laugh. I know he does.

His hands are on his hips, and he's staring at me intently.

"*Whoops.* Sorry, my hand slipped. I'm clum—"

He barrels toward me, cutting me off as he bends at the waist and hoists me over his broad shoulders.

I squeak in surprise, which is barely heard over the sound of Lucy's delighted laughter. "Wyatt, oh my God, put me down! You big… brute!"

He starts jogging around the field as if I weigh absolutely nothing. My fingers twist into the flannel material at his back, desperately trying to ignore the feel of his hard muscles and heated skin.

God, the man has always run hot.

"What are you doing?"

I try to lift my head to look around, but my hair is falling around my face, and I'm freaking upside down. All I can see is Lucy trailing behind us, laughing hysterically, her cheeks rosy and pink from the cold.

Wyatt's palm is dangerously close to my butt, trailing high on the back of my thigh as he holds me in place steadily.

"I swear to God, Wy—" The words die on my tongue as the world spins, and I land flat on my ass in the soft, fluffy snow in front of him, his large body caging me in while he hovers over me.

This ass just ... *tossed* me into the snow!

A murderous look passes over my face, and that only seems to make him grin harder. "Whoops, sorry, honey, I *slipped*. You know... clumsy and all that." He tosses me a cocky wink.

I grip a handful of fluffy snow in my palm and bring it to his face, rubbing it over every inch that I can get to before he laughs low and deep, the sound causing heat to pool in my belly. His fingers circle my wrist, pulling my hand away as he stares down at me, eyes burning into me.

I missed this. I missed *him*. Not just in a romantic way, but just... being around him.

We've always had the best times together, and even after all of the time that's passed, it seems like we could pick up right where we left off.

"Josie..." he starts, then trails off, gaze dropping to my lips and lingering there as I lick them, my breath forming a heated puff between us from the chilled air. The air around us thickens as time seems to slow.

He doesn't get to finish whatever he's going to say because Lucy drops down beside us, her bright green eyes dancing, "Daddy... Miss Josie... We won! Snowlene *won!*"

I might be hopeless at resisting the man who's always had my heart, but at least I can build a dang good snowwoman.

Josie

~~Reindeer Games~~

six

Team Rowdy Reindeers are killing the Christmas List competition.

In the last week, we've marked off the Wrapping Paper Runway and the Cookie Crawl, which was Lucy's favorite so far. To be fair, getting to spend the day making cookies, then eating them all at the end was a selling point for us too. We just finished with this afternoon's list task, deemed "Reindeer Games," with each contestant responsible for hosting a fundraising booth to benefit Strawberry Hollow at the town festival. Wyatt had the brilliant idea for us to make "Reindeer Food," which we sold out of almost immediately, putting us in first place and freeing us up to partake in the rest of the festival.

As much as it makes me nervous to admit... I'm enjoying spending time with both Lucy and Wyatt. I haven't had so much fun or laughed so hard in a really long time. And the scary part is how easily I could get used to this.

I know that my heart is teetering on a dangerously high ledge, the imminent threat of plummeting back into Wyatt's arms becoming more real by the second.

"Jos?" Wyatt's low timbre breaks through my thoughts, and I lift my gaze to where he's walking beside me with Lucy perched on his wide shoulders.

"Yes?"

"Luce wants to go ice-skating before we leave. Wanna come with us?" he asks.

I should probably say no to give myself some distance. I could easily find an excuse of needing to work on the stuff for school tomorrow, but the truth is I absolutely want to go with them.

So I nod, giving Lucy a wink when she squeals excitedly, her tiny hands fisting in Wyatt's already disheveled hair.

"Jeez, I'm going to be bald if you don't stop pulling my hair like that, bug." He groans as he reaches up to tickle her side playfully.

I lift the still-warm cup of hot chocolate to my lips and take a slow, savoring sip.

After Lucy catches her breath, she says with a serious expression, "Well, that's okay, Daddy. Grams says you'll be bald like Papa one day anyway."

The liquid in my mouth nearly comes spewing out when a look of sheer horror crosses Wyatt's face, and he stops outside the busy ice rink, lifting her from his shoulders and setting her onto her feet in front of him. "How about we just go skate and not talk about me losing my hair?"

She gives him a cheeky grin and pats the top of his unruly hair. "Suuuuure, Daddy."

Then she's prancing off toward the skate rental line, leaving Wyatt with his mouth agape. He stands to full height and drags a hand over his sharp jaw. "That girl."

"Oh, she is an angel."

"Yeah, one that's gonna make me skip getting grays and go straight to full-on bald." His words are a grumble, yet the corner of his full lips curve up.

He knows that she's got him wrapped around her little finger.

My shoulder brushes against his firm arm as we walk toward the rental line side by side, my gaze pinned on Lucy as she talks with another little girl her age while waiting for her turn.

"You look beautiful today, Josie. I like your sweater," Wyatt murmurs, his sudden admission taking me by surprise.

After the heated, nearly electric-charged moment at the snowman task, I thought we might talk about this... *feeling* between us. But he hasn't mentioned anything, focusing only on the tasks and Lucy, giving me that disarmingly handsome smile, constantly making my stomach feel as if there are flurries of lazy snowflakes falling in the pit of it.

I can feel the warmth of his gaze sliding over me as I clear my throat, pasting on a smile. "Uh... thank you. I just threw something *festive* on for school this morning." I say, glancing down at my Santa sweater.

"Well, you fit in perfectly here, then." He chuckles, gesturing around us.

Downtown has been transformed into a whimsical winter wonderland of sorts that only a place as magical as Strawberry Hollow could achieve. The scent of roasted chestnuts and sweet hot cocoa permeates through the air, the town Christmas tree standing tall and proud in the middle of Town Square. The boards of the ice skating rink are decorated with silvery strands of tinsel and garland, antique golden bells, and strings of warm white lights that cast a glow.

Every lantern that lines the sidewalk is tied with deep red, crushed velvet ribbons, and all of the businesses have transformed their storefronts with lights, wreaths, and garlands.

It looks like something out of a storybook, and standing with Wyatt Owens, my heart racing at his proximity... it *feels* like one.

"Josie Pearce, is that you?"

Turning, I see Wyatt's grams standing a few feet away, bundled up in a thick coat with a red-and-green plaid scarf around her neck. Her gaze flicks between Wyatt and me, a broad smile settling on her lips.

It's been forever since I've seen her, mostly because I've been actively avoiding anything to do with Wyatt until he showed up in my classroom.

I stiffen slightly. "Mrs. Owens, yes… hi!"

Wyatt chuckles beside me. "Grams, what are you doing here?"

"Oh, you know, I was going a bit stir-crazy at home with your papa, so I just thought I would get out of the house. I remembered the festival was today, so I just walked and shopped for a bit." She lifts the small bags in her hands. "Thought I would look for you guys and maybe take Lucy to see Santa? Give you two a bit to catch up… alone?"

Wyatt's gaze finds mine, a silent question passing between us, and I shrug.

I'm not sure that's the best idea, but I know that Lucy will probably be excited to go see Santa.

Although, that's her dad's call.

"Uh, sure, yeah, that would be great, Grams. Thank you."

She nods, her eyes twinkling as she glances between the two of us and then shoots me a wink before ambling off to Lucy.

We stand there together, watching as she tells Lucy she's taking her to see Santa. Obviously, she's over the moon, jumping on her tiptoes.

What five-year-old *wouldn't* be?

Now that we're completely alone, the air feels thicker, and my pulse seems to be racing faster, as if my body is suddenly aware that it's just the two of us.

"So…" I say, letting my words trail off.

Wyatt shakes his head, his unruly hair nearly falling across his forehead. "So…"

We walk down the sidewalk, my gaze moving up to the string of lights stretched above our heads through the town square. "Um… it's getting kind of late. I should probably head home." The excuse sounds weak, even as I say it.

I have nothing else I need to be doing, but being completely alone with Wyatt without Lucy as a buffer for the tension between us… it scares me.

"Or you could stay. And we could go ice-skating, get more hot chocolate, snow tube? Whatever you want," he says as he comes to a halt on the sidewalk, stepping closer until I feel the front of his boots touch mine. "Stay, Josie. I don't want you to leave."

His admission makes my heart sing, and although it's my job to protect it from getting hurt again, I find myself agreeing.

"Okay, I'll stay."

A small, shadowy look of surprise passes over his face. "Yeah?"

I nod as I draw my bottom lip into my mouth, ignoring the heat in my cheeks from his stare. "Yeah. I actually haven't been ice-skating in forever. Sounds like fun. And... I'll never pass up more of Edna's famous hot chocolate."

"Damn, Josie," Wyatt murmurs as he lifts a palm to his chest and rests it over his heart. "And here I was thinking you were staying just because you wanted to spend time with *me*."

"Maybe it's both."

His grin widens. "That's all I wanted to hear."

God, he's such a shameless flirt. Just as much now as he was back then.

Instead of responding, I roll my eyes, biting back the smile that I can't seem to pull from my lips. I almost forgot how easy it was to be around Wyatt, to laugh and flirt and to not have to think about guarding my heart.

Once we get to the skate rental booth, Wyatt tells the teenage attendant our skate sizes and then grabs them from her, giving her a smile that makes her eyes widen.

Clearly, I'm not the only one affected by how attractive he is. As if that wasn't enough, he's also charming and attentive, and all of it together is a lethal combination.

"You remember my shoe size?" I laugh as I take the worn skates from him and sit down on the bench to remove my boots.

His broad shoulder dips. "I told you I remember everything about you, Jos. I wasn't lying."

My God, how on earth am I supposed to be affected

by things like that when he says them? His sweet words unleash a flurry of wings in the pit of my stomach that makes my heart feel as if it's creeping up my chest into my throat.

A jarring reminder that even though time has passed, part of him is still the boy I once fell in love with.

I don't even know how to respond, so I just clear my throat, dropping my gaze down to the laces as my fingers fumble to get them tightened.

Partially because my gloves are thick and partially because I'm shaking slightly from a culmination of nerves and butterflies.

Wyatt moves to his knees at my feet, gently removing the laces from my trembling fingers. "Let me."

I swallow thickly while I nod.

His long fingers work quickly, getting my skate laced up in a matter of seconds, and then he's peering up at me with a lazy grin. "Do you remember the time we went skating down by Strawberry Falls with Jackson and Jude?" Rising to his feet, he offers me a hand, then pulls me to my feet when I slide my palm into his. "That day we played hockey and I took a puck to the face?"

"Oh God. Yes. I'm pretty sure I almost passed out from all of the blood." I shiver slightly at the memory. Although it's not entirely a pleasant memory, it's still one of my favorites. It was the first time he told me he loved me. Even though he was slightly out of it from the pain medicine, it still was the first time we both admitted that we were in love.

"You were the best nurse." Wyatt winks as we step out onto the slippery ice.

I almost lose my balance, the blade of my skate catching a rut in the ice, but Wyatt's arm flies out, wrapping around my waist to steady me. I can feel the heaviness of his palm curving along my hip, and it makes me shiver.

And it has nothing to do with the temperature.

"Uh, thank you. I told you... it's been a while. I'm a little rusty," I say as we glide along the ice.

His hand drops, but he doesn't put any distance between us, instead remaining so close that I can feel the heat of his body radiating onto me.

"I won't let you fall," he promises. "It's like riding a bike. Muscle memory. It's been... over eight years since I've been. Not a lot of ice-skating opportunities in California."

"I can't even *see* you as a California guy."

His dirty-blond brow arches. "Yeah? Why not?"

"I dunno..." I trail off as we skate around the rink, crisp, cool air hitting my cheeks. "I mean, I just can't see you sitting at a desk, working a nine-to-five, being a corporate kind of guy. I think I've always pictured you still on the ranch, covered in mud and sweat. Wearing boots and a hat. Not in a suit and tie."

Actually, now that I'm picturing it, I imagine he looked absolutely incredible in a suit.

"Yeah, it never really felt right to me either. That's why I ended up working for the petroleum company. Once I started consulting, I worked from home. No suits. Plus, it gave me freedom and flexibility, especially before Lucy was in school full-time." Chuckling, he skates ahead of me, then turns to face me, skating backward as he holds my eyes. "It feels good to be home at the ranch. Feels right."

It feels right to me that Wyatt's here too. Strawberry Hollow has *always* felt like where he belonged.

But I'm not going to say that out loud.

Because the most vulnerable part of me knows it's more than that. It's not just that he belongs here; it's that a part of my heart has always wanted him to come home to me.

I nod, attempting to focus on staying upright while skating and not how unnervingly handsome he is. "I'm… I'm glad you're home too, Wyatt."

Much more than I'm ready to admit.

Suddenly, a group of teenagers speeds past us, narrowly avoiding colliding with me, and it sends me pitching forward on the ice, directly into Wyatt's hard chest with an *oof*.

His arm slips around my waist, holding me steady, his massive body hardly jostled from our unexpected collision.

"Shit, are you okay?"

I nod, breathing heavily. "Yeah. God, that scared the crap out of me."

My heart is still racing in my chest as I lift my gaze to his. I'm pressed tightly against his body, my fingers tangled into the front of his shirt so tightly that I can feel the hard, sculpted muscles of his abdomen beneath the flannel. And now my heart is racing for an entirely *different* reason.

He's staring down at me, an unmistakable flicker of heat flaring in his warm brown eyes.

I allow myself for the briefest moment to imagine what it would be like having this version of Wyatt fitted between my thighs, his hard body moving over me, making my back arch in pleasure as his lips drag along my heated skin.

It's the last thing I should be thinking of, but the proximity and the scent of him surrounding me has my head swimming and my legs feeling wobbly. Like fresh citrus and cinnamon with a delicious hint of leather.

It's intoxicating.

His arm tightens around my waist, somehow pressing me harder against him, and my pulse thrashes wildly as his gaze drops to my mouth, lingering there for a moment.

And then he's leaning closer, so close that I can feel his breath fanning along my lips, centimeters away from me, and I'm pretty sure I've never wanted anything so badly as I want him.

My eyes flutter shut, and then his lips are on mine. His kiss is slow and unhurried, tentative almost, as he captures my lips, drinking down the small whimper that falls free.

That sound seems to push him over whatever edge he was teetering on because he lifts his palms to my jaw, cradling my face tenderly in his hands, and kisses me deeper, like he can't get enough, like it would never be enough.

My fingers tighten in his shirt, and when my tongue sweeps along the seam of his lips, he makes a deep, growly noise at the back of his throat, one that makes me tremble against him.

His tongue slides between my lips and tangles with mine, without hesitation.

God, he tastes exactly the way I remember, but the way that he kisses me now is different. It's raw and hungry. Young Wyatt's kisses made my heart flutter. But *this* man's kisses consume me wholly.

He tears his lips from mine, his chest heaving as he peers down at me through heavy, molten eyes.

Only then am I able to think slightly more clearly, my head having been dizzy with my want for him. It's then I realize we're surrounded by people, and the entire town probably knows that we just kissed like teenagers on the ice rink.

God, what am I doing? This is not a good idea.

I know that, and yet every time I'm around him, I just keep letting myself fall into everything that's Wyatt.

We're playing with fire, a dangerous game for my heart that's already been broken by this man once before.

And I know that if I'm not careful, *I'm* the one who's going to be burned.

Again.

 **seven**

There aren't many reasons I'll strip down and willingly jump into the frigid waters of Strawberry Falls in the dead of winter, but apparently, this damn competition is one of them.

And that I'm going to get to see Josie in a bathing suit when I've imagined her wearing less far too many times in the last three days since our kiss.

That damn kiss.

It's fucked with my head, and even when I've tried to stop thinking about it, about Josie, I couldn't.

She's invaded my every thought since that night, and hell, even invaded my dreams.

That kiss was… incredible. It was like coming *home*. So much more than I dreamed it would be, and I'm desperate for another one.

But after the kiss that night at the rink, she shut down, pulled away, and skated away so fast that I was worried she would trip. So honestly, I have no idea where her head is at or where things stand between us.

All I know is that I want her. Truly, despite all the years apart, I've never stopped wanting her.

That kiss only solidified what, deep down, I already knew: Josie's *mine*. She always has been. And if I have anything to do with it, she always will be.

Maybe she doesn't realize that yet or is too scared to admit it, but I'm going to do everything I can to prove to her that taking a second chance with me is worth it. There's no damn way that she doesn't feel the chemistry we have when we're together. It's even stronger now that we're no longer fumbling teenagers. And I know that I can't be the only one that feels this way.

I texted her earlier and asked if she wanted me to pick her up for tonight's task, but she thanked me and said that her brother offered to drop her off on the way to town. I know her well enough to know this is her way of creating distance between us.

Except that's the problem. All the time that's passed, all the miles and distance between us... still hasn't changed how it feels when we're together.

If anything, now it makes it feel like there's a magnetic pull drawing us closer.

I slam the door of my truck after parking in the lot outside of Strawberry Falls. I don't think I've ever seen it this packed before; nearly every spot is filled. I scan the parking lot for Josie, but I don't see her yet, so I put the towel under my arm and lock my truck before making my way down to the falls.

It's not quite dark yet, but the sun has begun to set, dusk settling over the sky. And with the sun going down, so has the temperature.

It's cold as shit out here. Why the hell are we doing a polar plunge at the coldest part of the day? My balls are shriveling just thinking about it.

On my walk down to the falls, a few guys from high school stop me for small talk, but I keep it short, my mind only on finding Josie.

Finally, I spot her talking to a friend we grew up with, Quinn Grant, a wide smile on her face.

I take a second to drink Josie in without her noticing. She's got on a fluffy red beanie, which covers her dark curls, and a big puffy jacket paired with black yoga pants that are fitted to her petite frame, tightly hugging the globes of her ass.

I can't help staring. She's so goddamn perfect it makes it hard to breathe.

How the hell did I ever walk away from her? Why didn't I try to keep her, no matter how hard it was going to be? And how the hell did I let all these years pass without trying to get her back?

Quinn leaves, so I cross the packed clearing toward the massive tent that's being used to ward off some of the cold pre-jump. When Josie finally spots me, her eyes widen slightly, and I smirk.

"W-Wyatt."

"Josie," I say, coming to a stop in front of her, my smirk widening into a full-blown smile when her pillowy lips part and a stuttering breath comes out. "You ready to do this?"

"Honestly? Not at all. I can think of about a hundred other things I'd rather be doing than jumping into that freezing water."

"Luce wasn't happy that she had to stay with Grams and Papa and miss all the fun. Then I reminded her how much she hates taking a bath, and she had nothing to say to that." I laugh. Tonight's task is an adult-only one, which seems smart because there was no way in hell I was letting my daughter jump into this cold-ass water. Josie's breath hitches as I step closer and grab her hand, dragging the pad of my thumb over the top of her knuckles in a languid sweep. "Don't worry, honey. I'll make sure to warm you up when it's over."

Fuck, I love the way her cheeks flush, turning the most delicious shade of pink. I want to see that flush travel the length of her body after I make her come.

"Alright, folks! The time has come," Mayor Davis says, voice raised over the chatter of the crowd.

Beneath his thick jacket, he's got on a pair of bright red swimming trunks that are made to look like Santa's suit, along with a matching shirt and hat, and I just shake my head because only this guy could pull off something so ridiculous and look like he was made to wear it.

"Tonight's list task is the annual Jingle Jump, which, as many of you already know, is Strawberry Hollow's polar plunge. Brrrr. Hence, the reason why we're at Strawberry Falls tonight." He chortles, tossing the crowd a wink. "This task is a simple one. You take a dip in the water when the air horn sounds, and then you can run back out. That's it. You'll be able to mark this task off your list and secure the points needed to move forward."

Sounds simple, but there's nothing simple about jumping into water that's got ice floating in it. Fuck, we're going to freeze.

But I'm pretty sure my daughter will never forgive me if I don't mark this off the competition list.

"Good luck!"

I glance at Josie, who's chewing the corner of her lip until it looks as if it'll bruise.

Reaching out, I drag my thumb gently along her bottom lip, pulling it from her teeth. "We don't have to do this, Jos."

She lifts her gaze to mine, the spot between her brows furrowing as her dark brow shoots up, "Of course we do. We can't let Lucy down!"

Of course she's worried about Lucy. The fact that it even matters to her, that she even cares enough to worry about my daughter, makes my heart squeeze in my chest.

I want to kiss her so fucking bad right now.

I want to show her how much it means to me that she cares about my daughter.

"Why are you looking at me like that?" she whispers.

I smirk. "Like what, Jos?"

Like I want to lay her out before me and kiss every inch of her until any protest she can think of has been washed from her mind.

She doesn't immediately respond, the column of her throat bobbing roughly as she swallows, then finally murmurs, "Nothing. I'm a little nervous. About the jump."

"Here's what we're going to do." I reach for her chin when she drops her gaze, tipping it up so I can look into her dark brown eyes. "I'm going to hold your hand, and we're going to jump together. It'll be cold as fuck, and we're going to be miserable, but I promise I won't let you go, okay, honey? Trust me."

I know that what I'm asking, even with something simple as jumping into the water, is probably a lot for her, but I *want* Josie to trust me again. I need to show her that I'm not going anywhere this time. That I'm not going to let go even when it's hard to hold on. Especially then. But words aren't enough, and I know that. I'm going to have to prove it to her.

"Okay," she whispers thickly, my stomach flipping with those two syllables. As simple as they are, they mean everything.

"Two-minute warning, folks!" Mayor Davis calls to the crowd, which means we're two minutes away from catching damn hypothermia, and I'm not looking forward to this.

It just goes to show that I'd do anything for my daughter.

I shrug out of my jacket, placing it on the tables that have been set up for the jump, and then tug the beanie off my head. Next, I reach behind my head and grasp the neck of my henley, pulling it off and immediately regretting it.

"Shit," I hiss when the cold air hits my bare torso, a frigid assault that sends a wave of goose bumps along my skin.

The only good part about this is being able to watch Josie slowly pull off her sweater after putting her puffy jacket next to mine on the table, leaving her in a strappy red bikini top that's stretched over her supple tits.

Fuck me.

My mouth nearly waters at the sight of her curvy, full hips. Hips that would fit perfectly in my hands. Tits that would fill my palms as if they were made for me.

And they *were* made for me. And *only* fucking me.

She's even more beautiful than I remember, the teenage version of her a distant memory that's now been replaced by a beautiful woman who has the ability to make me ache.

And I'm not the only one who's staring.

Josie's dark gaze does a slow, languid perusal of my chest, down to my abs, as she watches me flick the button of my jeans open and drag them down my hips, where they pool at my feet. I put on an old pair of swim trunks for today, and when her gaze lowers to my dick, her cheeks flush pink, creeping down her neck, and I chuckle lowly.

Her gaze whips to mine, and she shakes her head as if to clear it as she works on removing her yoga pants and boots. Her toes are painted the same red as her bikini, and the second she bends over to scoop up her shoes, giving me a better view of her tits, a groan almost bursts from deep in my chest.

The freezing-ass water isn't going to be as much torture as having her in front of me and not being able to touch her.

It's so fucking cold under this damn tent, even with the heat lamps, that she's already shivering, so I step forward and slide my arm around her shoulders, hauling her against my front.

Surprisingly, she doesn't protest, probably because she's a goddamn icicle and her teeth are chattering. "T-thank you."

Her skin's like fucking ice to the touch. I slide my palms up and down her arms to give her some warmth, and she sinks into my arms, burying her face against my chest.

I swear, I'd stand out here all damn night, letting my balls shrivel up, if it meant getting to hold her like this.

"In and out, honey. I've got you, okay? We're going to do it together," I rasp as I continue to run my palms down the raised flesh on her arms.

With another brief nod, we follow the rest of the crowd out to the water's edge. I swear it's so fucking cold walking on the snow-covered ground that the bottoms of my feet are numb.

I slip my hand in Josie's, lacing our fingers together and giving her the best smile I can manage that probably looks like more of a grimace, but fuck, I'm trying.

When the air horn sounds, I blow out a breath, take one last look at Josie, tightening my grip around her fingers, and then we jump.

The second we hit the water, the air wooshes from my lungs. It's so cold that it steals the breath from me, a shock to my entire body so powerful that I'm almost frozen in place for a second.

And then I kick my feet as hard as I can, pulling us to the surface because I'm not letting Josie go.

We break through the top of the water, both of us sucking in air, trying to fill our lungs, but damn, it's so cold it hurts.

I pull her to the water's edge and grab her by the waist, hoisting her onto the edge, then pull myself up, even though it feels like I'm frozen fucking solid. Somehow, the air hitting our already cold skin makes it even worse. Josie's teeth are chattering so hard I can hear them.

"C'mon," I murmur, pulling her into the tent and back under the heaters as I attempt to gather our clothing, my hands shaking from the cold. Opening the towels, I quickly put one around Josie's shoulders and wrap her up before putting mine on. "Let's go to my truck, get warm?"

She nods. "O-okay."

I toss my boots to the ground and step into them before bending over and scooping her into my arms bride-style, ignoring the layers of puffy jackets and clothes that are piled between us and the adorable squeak that tumbles out of her.

"W-wyatt! P-put me dow-w-n." She's trembling so hard that she can barely get the words out.

Of course, I don't listen because I'm not letting her freeze to death while walking to my truck. Instead, I just chuckle, my arms tightening around her body as I say, "Sorry, honey, can't do that."

We make it to my truck, and I deposit her directly onto the passenger seat along with the clothes, then walk around to the driver's side and slide into the seat. After I turn the truck on, the first thing I do is crank the heater all the way up, full blast.

Josie's using her jacket along with the towel that's

now damp and thus not offering much in terms of warming her up, so I turn to her. "C'mere, Jos."

For a second, she hesitates, shaking her head and pulling the jacket tighter around her.

I sigh. "Josie, you're freezing. Come use my body heat because I can't stand you shivering over there."

And because there's nothing more that I want than to have her in my arms again, in whatever way I can get her.

Finally, she huffs a sigh and throws the jacket to the floorboard. "Only because I'm freezing. That's it, Wyatt."

I can't stop the grin that curves my lips. "Sure, honey. Whatever you say."

Whatever she needs to tell herself to make herself feel better. I've got no qualms; I know exactly why I want Josie Pearce in my arms, and if it wouldn't scare her off like a wounded animal, I'd lay it all out for her.

She shoots me a pointed look that tells me to behave without actually saying a word before she pulls her towel off, letting it fall to the floor, and then climbs over the console of the truck into my lap. My arm circles her shoulders, pulling her against my chest, where, after the briefest moment of hesitation, she sinks into me with a content sigh.

I can't help that the first thing I notice is her taut, hardened little nipples pressing against the thin fabric of her bikini top. Fuck, I can almost make out her entire nipple, and I'm nearly aching to reach out and trace the wet fabric with my tongue.

I swallow, trying to push down the heady pull of arousal tugging at the base of my spine, but I know that it's useless. I've got her in my arms, perched on my lap like a present ready to be unwrapped, those tiny little red strings begging to be untied so much that trying to convince my dick that I don't want her is utterly pointless. It's a battle that I'm already losing as my gaze travels down her body to the small triangle of fabric between her thighs.

Fuck.

Josie lifts her gaze to mine, and the air seems to crackle between us as she blinks, heat flickering in her dark eyes. The tip of her pink tongue darts out to lick her lips, and the movement makes my dick twitch beneath her.

I watch as a swallow slides down her throat, her lips parting on a breathless hitch when she feels my erection hardening.

I can't fucking help it. The girl of my goddamn dreams is nearly naked in my lap, finally in my arms, and I'm hopeless in fighting this undeniable pull between us. A man is only so strong, and Josie Pearce is the biggest temptation I've ever faced.

She's always been the thread that's unraveled every part of me.

That never changed.

When she draws that plump pink lip between her teeth, moving her hips almost indecipherably, we both suck in a hiss as her ass brushes against my cock.

Her hooded gaze moves over my face as she lets out a trembling breath.

I can almost *see* the moment that the decision clicks behind her eyes, and she's whispering, "Fuck it."

And then she slams her lips against mine, twisting in my lap until her knees are fitted on either side of my hips, hands flying to my nape as she moans against my mouth.

A deep groan vibrates in my throat while I thread my hands in her hair, tangling in the still-wet strands, pulling her impossibly closer to me.

She tastes like perfection. Like the sweetest treat on the planet.

Like *mine*.

We're a flurry of frantic, desperate moves, clashing teeth, soft whimpers, both of us too lost in the moment to even care that we're in my truck in the parking lot, surrounded by half the people in the town.

Every rock of her hips, every brush of her taut nipples against my bare skin, sends my head swimming. Her warm center in that tiny bikini presses tightly against me. My cock is so hard that it might bust through my fucking pants at any moment.

Josie nibbles on my bottom lip, biting it gently before letting it go with a breathy sigh. My palms slide up her back, pressing her tighter against me as I kiss along the edge of her jaw, memorizing every single inch of her that I can feel.

"Wyatt…" She pants my name like a prayer. "I…"

I pull back, breathing heavily as I stare up at her.

Her throat bobs as she whispers thickly, her heated gaze hitting me full force. "Take me home."

"Are you sure?"

Without hesitation, she nods. "I'm sure."

Josie

eight

There's not a lot of things that I'm sure of right now. My feelings about Wyatt, the future, what all of this means for both of us.

But what I am sure of is that I *want* him.

Desperately.

God, I feel like I'm going to combust if I don't feel his skin on mine, if we don't finish what we've started. After that kiss the night at the Reindeer Games and then tonight's moment in his truck that left me trembling with pent-up need, I feel like my body is on *fire*. Like it would only take one touch for every part of me to go up in a fiery inferno of desire.

I shut the front door behind me, flicking the lock shut, turning back to press myself against the cool wood. Wyatt's massive body takes up so much space in my small, cozy living room as he bends in front of the unlit fireplace, adding another log inside of it.

Even with the heat on, there's a slight chill hanging in the air, but right now, with the way that my skin is humming with anticipation, I can hardly even tell.

Wyatt never put his clothes back on after the Jingle Jump, too focused on getting me into his truck, and now that he's standing here wearing nothing but a pair of tight swim trunks, my gaze moves over him in a slow perusal, drinking in every inch that I've missed since he's been gone.

He's raw masculinity.

Tall, broad, powerful, sculpted in ways that I can hardly even wrap my mind around.

He's... *gorgeous*.

The defined muscles of his back seem to ripple as he moves the wood around inside the fireplace, and a jolt of desire pulses through me so hard that my breath catches.

I press my thighs together in an attempt to dull the throb that's building between them, to no avail.

Wyatt's gaze flits to mine, his mouth twitching when he sees me nearly panting against the front door.

It's been... a while since I've been with anyone.

And truthfully, since he's come back to town, I can't even recall how many times I've gone back and forth in my head with this same scenario. I tried convincing myself it was a bad idea, tried to think of as many excuses as I could to talk myself out of it.

But everything kept coming back to the fact that I

want him, and none of those excuses held up against the war with my heart and mind.

"C'mere, Josie," he rasps. Those four syllables send a wave of goose bumps erupting along my flesh and a shiver traveling down my spine.

Swallowing down the tightness in my throat, I push off the door obediently, crossing the room one slow step at a time until I'm in front of him.

So close that I can see the newly lit flames from the fireplace dancing in his bourbon-colored irises, which are framed by dark lashes. His eyes seem to smolder, just like the fire.

"Do you know how many times I've thought about this moment?" he breathes, reaching out and sweeping the rough pads of his fingers along the bare skin of my shoulder, slipping beneath the strap of my bikini top. "How many times in the last two weeks that I've come with your name on my lips? I'm fucking crazy about you, Josie."

Oh God.

Slowly, he tugs the strap off my shoulder, then repeats the motion with the other, never lowering his gaze, never taking his eyes off mine, and somehow, that only makes the simple movement so much more intense. More intimate.

More… something that I'm too afraid to admit to myself.

Ignoring the swell in my chest, I step forward and

slant my mouth over his as I lift up on my tiptoes and tangle my fingers in the hair along his nape, unable to last another second without touching him.

The frantic desperation that we felt in the truck earlier has been reignited, and his rough hands are suddenly everywhere, sliding down the bare, heated skin of my back, his fingers dancing along the notches of my spine, down to the curve of my ass, where he groans against my lips, low and deep.

Like he couldn't help the sound vibrating out of him, an involuntary reaction to the feel of me in his hands.

Quite possibly the sexiest sound I've ever heard.

His tongue sweeps between my open lips, demanding access, stroking and flicking against mine in a way that I feel all the way from my throbbing clit to the tips of my toes, a full-body reaction to simply being *kissed* by this man.

The tips of his fingers dig into my ass as he effortlessly lifts me off my feet. My legs wrap around his waist, and I feel his hard erection brushing against my aching core, causing me to whimper.

My entire body feels like a live wire, and I have no doubt that a few touches from Wyatt would send me over the edge. My fingers curl into his hair, tugging when his teeth scrape along my bottom lip.

With each breath, his lips trail along the edge of my jawline, down to my neck, where his tongue flicks out, sucking at the sensitive skin of my pulse point.

Lower.

And lower.

He kisses a path along my body to my chest, dragging his tongue along my skin as he tastes me. My eyes flutter shut, heat flooding my lower belly as he trails lower and lower until he meets the heaving swell of my chest.

Only then do my eyes fly open, connecting with his hooded gaze as he closes his lips over my nipple through the fabric of the bikini. Even with a barrier, it has me moaning breathlessly, tugging tightly at the strands of his hair, my back arching and pushing myself further into his mouth.

I feel the rough scrape of his teeth over the taut, impossibly pebbled peak, and my head swims.

"Wyatt," I whimper, hardly recognizing my own voice, which is heavy with need. I twine my fingers tighter in his hair as he lowers us to the thick rug before the fireplace and spreads me out beneath him. His heated gaze rakes over my body in a way that has me pulsing, heart racing, head dizzy with need.

"You're the most beautiful thing I've ever seen," he murmurs quietly, lifting his eyes to mine.

I feel the same about him.

Drawing my swollen bottom lip between my teeth, I reach for him, placing his hands back along the expanse of my stomach and slowly sliding them higher until his big, rough palms are cupping my breasts.

The eye contact between us is so intense that it makes me ache between my legs and somewhere beneath my breastbone.

"Touch me, Wyatt."

I watch as the thick column of his throat bobs, the muscles of his shoulders tight with restraint. But I don't want him to be restrained. I want the uncontrolled Wyatt. The one I've never experienced.

"Don't hold back. *Please,*" I whisper thickly as I trail my fingers along the hard plane of his stomach, ghosting them along the dips between his abs, lower until I'm brushing along his cock, which is impossibly hard beneath the swim trunks.

He hisses, a low grunt vibrating out of his chest when I curve my palm over his length.

God, he's… so much bigger than I remember?

Wyatt's hips fit between my thighs as he slips his hand beneath my back and deftly unties my bikini top, pulling it free and tossing it to the side.

"*Fuck,*" he drawls, his blown pupils raking along my chest at the same time he cups my breast in his palm, rolling the taut, pebbled peak of my nipple between his fingers. "You were made for my hands, honey."

The words wash over me, praise that I never knew I sought until now.

Lowering his mouth, he closes his lips around my nipple, sucking the bud deep and flicking the sensitive peak with this tongue until I'm nearly panting beneath him.

Until I'm delirious with need, my head dizzy from the delicious assault of his mouth along my skin.

Wyatt blazes a path down my stomach, leaving hot, wet kisses along my skin until he makes it to my navel, dipping his tongue in and then dragging it to the waistband of my bikini bottoms.

My heart is thrashing in my chest in sync with the wild, erratic pounding of my pulse.

Part of me can't even believe this is *happening* right now. But an even bigger part of me is just thankful that it is. That I get this experience with Wyatt no matter what happens after tonight.

I refuse to let my head really go there right now, instead forcing my attention to the man who's hovering over me, heat burning in his honey-steeped eyes.

With his gaze pinned on mine, he presses soft, achingly tender kisses along the inside of my thighs, moving closer and closer to my throbbing core.

God, I've never wanted something as badly as I want Wyatt's hands on me, his mouth, his fingers, *all* of him.

When his lips ghost along the damp fabric of my bikini, my back arches from the rug, and he lets out a nearly pained grunt.

"Already wet for me, honey?" It doesn't seem like he's asking a question, more making an observation, but I find myself nodding anyway, watching as his pillowy lips tug upward in a devastating smile. "What a good girl."

My clit throbs at the praise. I'm not even sure when it became something I liked this much.

But then again... this is *Wyatt*.

There's a soft brush of his lips as he hooks a finger in the string of my swimsuit bottoms and, with one tug, has the strings falling free, leaving me completely bare for him. The heat from the fire warms my skin, but it's nothing like the inferno that's building inside of me.

His admiring gaze moves over my core as his lips part, and his tongue wets his lips.

Is there anything more attractive than a man staring at the most intimate part of you while looking as if he could devour you whole?

Wyatt's fingers sweep along my already wet center as he spreads me open and rasps, "Pretty and perfect as I remember."

Lowering his mouth to me, he slowly flicks the tip of his tongue over my clit, my back bowing completely off the rug.

And then he flattens his tongue and drags it through my wet center in the most torturously slow way I've ever experienced. It's maddening, the unhurried way he's taking his time, savoring it, lapping at me until my hands are flying to his hair and tugging roughly at the strands in desperation to hold on to something, to ground myself. To bring my head back from the clouds I feel as if I'm currently floating on.

Holy... crap.

"Oh... God," I pant, my voice wavering as the words break. "*Wyatt...*" A handful of ragged syllables strung together.

His low chuckle vibrates against my wet core, sending another heady burst of pleasure soaring through my already heavy limbs. "Watch me eat your pretty little pussy, honey. Watch me eat you like I've dreamed about doing for so fucking long."

I manage to keep my eyes open if only to drink in the sight of this beautiful man fitted between my legs, my thighs thrown over his broad, tan shoulders, and his tongue buried inside of me.

My hips squirm when he circles my entrance with his fingers and slowly, inch by inch, sinks two of them inside me at the same time he swirls his tongue on my clit. I raise them to meet the pace of his fingers, the flick of his tongue, pulling him against me by his hair in a way that I worry I might hurt him, but his growl of approval is all that I need to know that he is just as lost to this as I am.

I watch Wyatt slip his other hand into the front of his swim shorts and palm his cock, slowly pumping his fist.

It's so erotic, watching him be so turned on from just tasting *me* and giving *me* pleasure.

The tug in my lower belly pulls taut as my orgasm builds, and Wyatt never stops the sweep of his tongue. He sucks my clit and licks me through every second of the intense pleasure throbbing through me.

"Don't stop," I plead deliriously.

All it takes to send me spiraling into the most powerful orgasm of my life is him closing his lips around my clit and sucking, alternating pressure. He strokes the spot inside of me that has my toes curling on his shoulders and tiny black spots dancing behind my eyes that are squeezed so tightly shut my head swims.

"Wyatt, Wyatt, Wyatt," I chant on a desperate breath, my legs beginning to tremble as my core tightens and clenches, my mind spinning as I give myself over to my climax.

"That's my girl," he pauses to whisper against my heated flesh. "So fucking good for me, Josie. Soaking my tongue, coating my beard with your cum."

His filthy words, something new present-day Wyatt excels at, wash over me as the aftershocks of my orgasm pulse through me. He never stops, wringing every ounce of pleasure out of me until I'm limp, completely sated and boneless.

And then he rises above me, a wolfish grin on his too-handsome face, and murmurs, "Give me *another*, honey."

~~Gingerbread Gala~~

nine

Josie's heated, heavy-lidded eyes peer up at me as I hold myself above her, my forearm planted on the soft fur of the rug beneath us and the pad of my finger tracing a rosy pink nipple illuminated by firelight.

Fuck, I've dreamed of this very moment so many times, her laid out beneath me with a halo of dark hair spread around her, her sated expression after I devoured her.

A breathy moan pushes past her lips, and her hips rock, brushing against my cock, which is already weeping after just… *tasting* her.

"I can't get over how stunning you are, Josie," I murmur, rolling her taut nipple between my fingers, never taking my eyes off hers. "Fucking perfection."

Even in just the dim light of the fire, I see her cheeks turn pink, and I grin.

I continue to tease her nipples with my fingers and my tongue, flicking the tip over each peak until she's squirming against me again, the smallest movement that has a heady dose of arousal trickling down my spine.

My hips snap forward, sending my cock jutting against her pussy, which is still glistening from her orgasm, and a soft whimper pushes past her lips. Her hands fly to my shoulders, her nails creating crescents on my skin from how tightly she's planted her fingers.

"Wyatt..." The breathless moan has my balls tightening.

"I love when you say my name like that, honey. Fuck. I want you to *scream* it while my cock is buried inside of you."

Her eyes darken as she draws her plump, thoroughly kissed bottom lip between her teeth and gives me a wicked smile. "Then get inside of me, *honey*."

I've seen many different versions of the woman beneath me, but the bold, confident, ask-for-what-she-wants version? Yeah, I think it just might be my favorite.

Shit, I'm so crazy about her. Out of my mind for her. Anticipation and raw desire course through me as her hips roll, trying to press her pretty pink little pussy against my straining erection.

A low hum vibrates in my throat when she flattens her hands along my abdomen and slowly trails her fingers lower, the muscles coiling and tightening from her touch.

I'm nearly shaking, my control fraying at the edges, the moment her hand slips beneath the waistband of my shorts and she curves her soft palm over my dick, squeezing tightly.

All while holding my gaze in a way that somehow feels more intimate than any moment we've ever shared together before.

Fuuuuuuck.

The sharp hiss that bursts from my throat echoes into the living room around us as she pumps my cock, sweeping her thumb over the head and gathering the precum, spreading it around and coating me.

There's no way I'm lasting when I finally get inside of her. Not when I've been desperate for this, desperate for her, for so fucking long.

Josie Pearce will be my undoing. One that I will gladly accept.

I reach between us and drag my fingers through her pussy, coating my fingers with her creamy arousal before slipping them inside of her, using the pad of my thumb to circle her clit while I stroke her G-spot.

My gaze moves over her pliable body, admiring how easily my touch sets her on fire. Her back bows from the rug, and she cries out.

She's already ready for me, but I want to play with

her, get her writhing beneath me before I slide my cock inside of her.

Her pussy's so damn pretty as she stretches around me, greedily pulling me in.

It only takes a few thrusts before she's lifting her hips to meet my fingers. My hips flex into her hand of their own accord, my body rolling to meet the tight pump of her fist as she works me.

I'm fucking dizzy with how badly I need her.

I slip my fingers out of her, and her eyes fly open in protest. I just smirk as I bring them to my mouth and suck her juices off them as hungrily as I'd eaten her little pussy, cleaning every last drop.

"God, Wyatt, please, fuck me," she moans. "Now."

Hearing her begging me to fuck her is the true end of my restraint, the unraveling string now snapped into something desperate.

Together, we yank my shorts down my hips, and I manage to pull them off. The tip of my cock drags through her wetness in the process, causing us to both groan in unison.

"I need to grab a con—"

Josie shakes her head, stopping me. "I'm covered, if you're okay with it…"

Holy fucking hell. Sliding inside of her… bare?

There's no way this is going to last long with this being the first time we've been together in eight years.

I'm going to come as fast as I did when I was a damn teenager.

Shoving a rough swallow down my throat, I nod, gripping the base of my cock. "I'm good too. Are you sure?"

I don't take my eyes off her, needing to not just hear the affirmation in her words but also see it in her eyes.

This is important to me, to *us*, and I'm determined to get it right this time.

Her face softens. "I'm *sure*, Wyatt." Emotion shines back at me, and it tells me everything I need to know. That this moment means as much to her as it does to me.

My exhale is a shudder as my fist tightens around my cock, and I drag it through her folds, coating the head of it with her arousal and bumping it against her clit before lining up with her entrance. I push forward the slightest amount, barely even a breath, and the head of my cock slips inside.

Her breath hitches, and I lower my mouth to hers, capturing her lips and swallowing down her moan as the wet, tight heat of her pussy envelops my cock. Pleasure bursts behind my eyes as I slowly thrust inside of her until I'm buried to the hilt, so deep that I lose track of where she ends and I begin.

I pause, giving her a second to adjust, but I never stop kissing her, our tongues tangling together feverously.

I pull back, staring down at her, trying to memorize every single second of this moment. My gaze catalogs her swollen lips, her stuttering breath, the pretty pink flush of her cheeks, her pebbled nipples.

She's a vision, an actual fucking dream.

She's *mine*.

When I feel her nails bite into my back, I withdraw and slowly sink inside of her again, this time rolling my hips and watching as her eyes roll back and she arches, pushing herself further down on my cock.

The rough pad of my thumb finds her clit, and I circle it in slow, deliberate motions as I set a pace of thrusts, slow and deep, each one harder than the last.

Being inside of her without a barrier, a feeling we've never experienced together in the past, and it's *indescribable*.

Euphoria like I've never imagined existed.

"Fuck, honey, you feel so good wrapped around me," I rasp, my voice hoarse with need.

Josie's hands slide down the expanse of my back to my ass, where she pulls me deeper into her, hitching her leg higher on my side. "Tell me what you need."

Her words tumble out breathlessly. "More. Please."

I strum her clit faster as she clings to me, my thrusts turning hard, deep, quick, both of us barreling towards a climax that I already know is going to change my life. That's going to change the trajectory of every thought I have. Permanently.

"Come for me, honey. Milk my cock so I can come inside of you," I pant, flexing my hips deep and rolling them, reaching resistance. "I want to watch it drip out of you."

"Don't stop," she pleads on a trembling breath. "Please, don't stop."

"I'm never stopping, honey. Let go. Come for me."

I feel the familiar tug in my spine, my balls drawing tight and desperate for release. The moment I feel Josie's pussy tighten around me, pulling me impossibly deeper into her as her orgasm surges through her, I come on a ragged grunt, my fingers digging into the soft flesh of her hips. I fill her pussy with every drop of my cum as she spasms so tightly around me that my vision dances while she cries out my name over and over and over.

My thrusts slow into a languid rock of my hips, unable to break the physical connection between us as I stare down at the beautiful woman beneath me who looks as thoroughly fucked as I feel.

"Wow," she says after a moment. "That was..."

"Everything," I supply for her, stilling inside of her. Dipping my head down, I press a sweet, lingering kiss to her mouth, to the corner of her lip, the tip of her nose, and lastly, her forehead. Gently, I pull out of her, already mourning the loss of feeling her wrapped around me. "That was *everything*, Josie."

We stay just like this for a moment, just breathing

together, soaking in the quiet stillness of what just happened.

Until I lower myself onto my side and ghost my fingers along the center of her chest, over her tit to her peaked nipple, circling it.

Her dark eyes hold mine as she grins, sitting up and pushing me onto my back on the rug and straddling my cock, which is still glistening with our shared release.

"Now... it's my turn."

Wyatt

"Your snowman looks like it has a *dick*, you idiot."

One thing that seems to have stayed exactly the same while I was gone is that the Pearce household is and probably always would be pure chaos.

Sitting here surrounded by Josie's older brothers, her parents, and now Jackson's new fiancée, Emma, it feels just like the time I spent here when we were teenagers. Except instead of letting her brothers give her shit, Josie Pearce is giving it right back, and I've never been so proud of my girl.

Lucy giggles. "Daddy, he said di—"

Josie puts her hand over her mouth, cutting Lucy off from repeating what her brother Jude said while shooting him a look that says she might actually kill him.

I chuckle, and then she pins the same look on me, so I promptly snap my mouth shut.

"Jude, I swear to Saint Nicholas himself, if you don't watch your mouth, I'm making you leave!" Josie warns as she drops her hand from Lucy's mouth. "Ma, tell him, please."

Josie's mom narrows her gaze at Jude, lifting a brow. "She's right. We've got a little one here tonight, so I expect all of you to watch your mouths. Not *just* Jude."

Her pointed gaze even drags to mine.

Damn, Mama Pearce is still as fierce as she was back then. Soft on the outside and sweet as anyone I'd ever met, but when you push her... well, I wouldn't actually know because I knew better back then, and I sure as hell know better now.

"Jos, Wyatt, want another glass of eggnog?" Emma calls from the doorway, lifting a glass.

I shake my head. "Nah, I've got to drive, but thank you." Josie looks hesitant, like she's worried about saying yes, so I lean forward and dip my head toward her ear. "Have another glass, honey. I'll drive you home."

When my lips brush against the shell of her ear, she trembles. "I-I'll have one. Thank you, Emma." Her words are slightly breathless, making me grin.

I pull back, entirely too fucking pleased that I have her cheeks flushed.

"Hey, Lucy, do you think you could help me carry

the cookies we made in here?" Mama Pearce asks her, and she nods enthusiastically, bounding out of her chair to follow her into the kitchen.

The second she's gone, Josie turns to me, peering through her thick lashes as she leans forward. "*Behave, Wyatt Owens.*"

And then I feel her hand slowly sliding along the top of my jean-clad thigh toward my cock, and my knee shoots up, banging noisily against the underside of the kitchen table. All of the gingerbread supplies on top jostle with the motion, and every single one of her brothers turns to stare at us.

Fuuuuuck.

Josie shifts beside me, giggling quietly, and I shoot her a pointed glare. This damn girl.

She makes me crazy. Crazy about her, crazy *because* of her.

The last thing I want is all of her wild-ass brothers on me because I'm getting hard for their baby sister under the damn gingerbread table.

A few minutes later, Lucy and Mrs. Pearce, followed by her husband, Ed, stride through the entryway carrying a platter of cookies. Lucy's face is bright with excitement as she plucks one off the top after setting it on the kitchen table and rushes over to me.

"Look, Daddy, I made this one!" She holds up what I think is… an elf? Maybe riding a reindeer? It's frosted with a handful of sprinkles on the bottom part only.

Not sure, but either way, she's so damn proud of it.

"Great job, bug," I say as I lean forward and take a bite out the side. "Mmmm. Tastes as good as it looks."

I hear Josie laughing beside me, and Lucy turns to her, offering her the rest of the cookie. She takes a bite, moaning around a mouthful. "Wow, Lucy, I think you might make the *best* cookies ever."

"Really?" Lucy asks, unable to keep the excitement from her words. "You mean it?"

Josie nods. "Yes, definitely."

She's always encouraging Luce and making her feel great about the things she does, and fuck, it makes me fall for her a little more each time. Every time I see her interacting with my daughter is like a shot directly to my heart. She's genuine and kind and clearly cares about her, whether I'm around or not.

It means everything to me, and I want her to know it.

"Are you ready to build our gingerbread gala submission?" Josie asks her, leaning forward and tucking a stray piece of Lucy's strawberry blonde hair that's escaped from her braid out of her eyes. "This one is worth two points, so we've gotta work reallllly hard."

Lucy's expression sobers as she nods. "Yes. I'm going to be extra careful."

"That's my girl," Josie says. "Me and your dad can get started on the super-hard part, but then it's up to you to help me put it all together."

Before Lucy can respond, Jude cuts in. "Hey, Luce? Wanna help me with the gumdrop garland? I've gotta make sure I have a better gingerbread house than Josie because I always beat her, every year. Not very fair she has you helping her out."

Lucy's lips curve into a cheeky smile that shows her missing front tooth, and Josie's eyes roll, but I can see that she's trying not to smile at Jude's constant teasing.

Not only is tonight a task to check off of the competition list, but for as long as I can remember, the Pearce family has had an annual gingerbread house family competition, so a submission for the Gingerbread Gala being on the list this year worked out perfectly.

Two gingerbread competitions, one house.

Of course, all of the Pearces have easily fallen to Lucy's charm. She is the cutest kid on the planet, even though I guess I'm slightly biased. It's nice to have Lucy be around them because they've always been a tight-knit family. Even back when I was a teenager, every time I was here, I always felt like I was right at home.

I fit right into the chaos, and I loved it then.

And I love it still. It's only a bonus that now my daughter gets to be here too.

"Not sure you want me to do the building part, Jos," I whisper next to her ear once Lucy runs off to help Jude, leaving us alone at our end of the table. Josie's slightly bent over the blank canvas of gingerbread, the corner of her bottom lip pulled between her teeth as she focuses in intense concentration. "My fingers are better used in other places."

Her eyes widen, and her head whips to me as I lean back slightly. "You are incorrigible, Wyatt, my gosh."

I chuckle. "Can't help it. You make me that way. I can't stop thinking about the other night, honey. The way you rode my co—"

My words die on my tongue as she shovels a handful of sprinkles in my mouth, her brown eyes wide and her cheeks stained pink.

"Wyatt!" she sputters.

If her eyes hadn't darkened and her chest wasn't slightly heaving, I might be convinced she's mad, but nah, my girl's turned on.

Hell, I am too, just thinking about the entire night I spent making her come until she was a limp mess beneath me, unable to even hold her eyes open. Fuck, she was magnificent. A work of art that no one will ever fucking see the way I did ever again.

"God, you two are making me nauseous," Jackson complains gruffly. I glance over and see Emma elbowing him in the side, and he lets out a grunt. "Fuck, baby, they are!"

"I mean, he's not wrong," Jude quips from his side of the table. "I never thought I'd see the day again where you were back together. Good thing we all love Wyatt."

Josie opens her mouth to speak, then snaps it shut as her gaze cuts to Lucy. "We're... That... We're not together. We're just friends. Doing the Christmas List competition."

Even though we haven't defined *us*, and I haven't wanted to push too hard after the other night and make her retreat... it still stings hearing that we're only friends coming out of her mouth.

Not when it feels like so much more.

When whatever's happening between us feels like *everything*.

"Y'all leave Josie alone now. Quit being nosy," Mr. Pearce interjects before anyone else can add to the conversation, and I watch as immediate relief floods Josie's face. She goes back to working on her gingerbread without sparing me another glance.

As much as I want to have this talk, I know now is not the time or place to have it, so I get to work adding the icing to pieces of the gingerbread house.

I also wasn't bullshitting when I said this is not my strong suit, and most of the icing ends up on the table rather than the gingerbread.

It doesn't take long before Josie's groaning. "Wyatt, you realize that the icing goes on there, right?" Lifting a brow, she gestures to the cookie that's admittedly a fucking mess.

"I'm aware, honey, but I don't have a steady hand," I say, cocking my head. "I could watch?"

She huffs. "No, we have to work together. There's no way I can finish this thing by myself."

Lucy is still working with Jude, and every time I look up at her, she seems to be sneaking another gumdrop into her mouth. I already warned her once that she's going to end up with a stomachache if she doesn't stop eating so much sugar.

Then Josie got this dreamy look on her face, sighing with a sweet smile. "You're adorable when you're being a cute, protective daddy."

Clearly, she doesn't think I'm still adorable now since I seem to be fucking up our chances of winning the Gingerbread Gala.

"Here, why don't you work on the roof," she says, pushing a small slab of chocolate my way. "Just put little lines that will make it look like shingles."

My brow arches, and she sighs. "Just try, Wyatt."

I almost forgot how competitive Josie could be, and I can't stop the smile that splits my face. "You got it, *honey.*"

Working with the chocolate seems to be a little easier, so I find myself focused on the roof for several minutes. Once I'm finished, I get a glance of approval and a hint of a smile from Josie, so apparently, I didn't fuck up this part too.

Lucy comes back over to our side of the table, helping Josie line the front of the gingerbread house with small bushes that she fashioned out of colored icing.

It's actually starting to look like a house, which is surprising because every time I attempted to do this with Lucy in the past, I had a pile of iced gingerbread that we ended up eating just so it didn't go to waste.

"Looks good, Jos," I praise, taking to watching her put the finishing touches on the house. She glances over at me, my pulse racing when she gives me a sweet smile, her brown eyes lighting up.

"Thank you. It might actually be a winner. What do you think?"

I nod. "Of course."

"Josie, what the hell is that?" Jensen blurts from across the table, his gaze trained on Josie's gingerbread house.

Oh shit.

"What do you mean, what is that, Jensen? It's a gingerbread house," Josie says slowly, her eyes narrowed.

Jensen balks, lifting a dark brow. "Yeah, it looks like a brothel. Shit, sorry. A b-r-o-t-h-e-l," he spells when Mrs. Pearce pins a pointed stare at him.

"Oh my God. Jude, cover Lucy's ears."

Jude reaches up behind Lucy and covers her small ears with his large hands, her toothless grin widening as she looks between Josie and Jensen.

"Jesus Christ, Jensen! It's the house from *Home Alone*, you... twat!" Josie cries.

I bring my fist to my mouth to cover my laugh, feigning a cough because I do not want the wrath of Josie Pearce right now. Apparently, Jensen has zero self-preservation because Josie is turning red with how mad she is. She just spent the last two hours working on that gingerbread house, only for her brother to tell her it looks like a damn brothel.

Which is funny as hell, but I'm never going to admit that out loud.

"Yeah, that's the *Home Alone* house if Marv and Harry were *pimps*, sis," he scoffs.

Motherfucker.

Josie goes deathly still, her jaw set in a firm, tense line. I'm unsure of what's going to happen next mostly because, well, my daughter's present, and as sweet and gentle as my Josie girl is, she has her spitfire moments, and this sure as hell seems like one.

Finally, after the longest, most uncomfortable silence in the history of Christmas, Josie smiles. A wide grin that overtakes her entire face. "You know, Jensen... This is a family Christmas activity, so I'm going to refrain from saying what I'm thinking of saying, but I think now is as good of a time as any to tell Mom and Dad about your *new* girlfriend."

Jensen's eyes widen, and I watch as he visibly gulps.

"Jensen Pearce, new girlfriend? You have a new girlfriend that you didn't tell us about? You know I've been telling you that I'm not getting any younger, and as the oldest of my boys, I hoped you'd settle down soon and give me some grandkids, and this whole time, you've been seeing someone... in secret?" Mrs. Pearce says with surprise written on her face. She brings a hand to her heart and clutches it.

"Ma, I'm sor—" he starts, but Josie cuts him off with a saccharine grin.

"Oh, and did I mention his new *older* girlfriend?"

Shots fired.

"Josie, God d—" he begins, but Josie throws a piece of gingerbread at him, where it lands with a splat on the front of his shirt. Promptly cutting him off.

"I *told* you to stop cursing in front of Lucy!" she says.

He shakes his head. "I wasn't going to fu— Her ears are still covered!"

I'm watching the exchange between both of them alongside Jackson and Emma, who are both holding back their laughter, shaking their heads.

"Can I uncover my ears now?" Lucy says, and we all lose it. The breaking point of the chaos is my daughter, and it's the perfect icebreaker for the tension between Jensen and Josie.

She has zero idea what's going on, but she joins in with the laughter until Jameson scoops her off her feet and holds her in the air like an airplane as he runs around the kitchen.

And it's right now that I realize how important this moment is, both for me and Lucy. How much we fit in with the Pearce family and how right it feels to be here again with Josie at my side along with my daughter.

It feels like this year is going to be the best Christmas I've ever had.

Both of us at home in Strawberry Hollow.

With Josie.

Josie

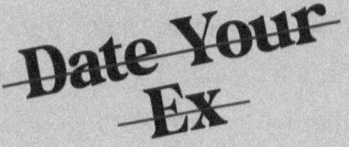

ten

I honestly can't even *remember* the last time I went on a date. An actual date that wasn't at the hands of my mother, trying yet again to set me up with one of the poor, unsuspecting guys from town.

Which makes me even more nervous about tonight.

Both that it's been forever since I've been on one and because I'm going on a date with *Wyatt*.

An official, *real* date. For the first time since we were teenagers.

Or a holidate, as he's calling it, since Christmas is less than two weeks away.

I have absolutely no idea what he has planned, and that does nothing to help the swirl of nerves dancing in the pit of my stomach. He just said to dress warm, which probably means that whatever we're going to be doing is something outdoors.

Truthfully, the last few days have seemed like a dream. A dream that I'm terrified if I hold on too tightly, it'll disappear like a cloud of smoke within my grasp.

I've been asking myself the same questions over and over, somehow expecting the answer to magically come to me like a Christmas miracle: *Could I give my heart to Wyatt again? After everything we've been through? Could I chance being hurt by the man who has more power than anyone has ever held over my heart? Will it last this time?*

When I hear the low rumbling of his truck pulling into the driveway, I take one last look in the mirror at my reflection, hoping that the outfit I picked for tonight is perfect.

I'm wearing my favorite pair of blue jeans tucked into a pair of knee-high tan boots and a cream-colored sweater that always complements my skin tone and hair color, all paired with my tan trench coat that falls just above my knees. And a dark brown beanie with a fuzzy pom-pom on the top, not only because I love the color and it goes great with the outfit I chose but also because it is freaking freezing, and I don't want to spend the entire night with frozen ears.

My dark curls are styled into loose waves that fall to my waist, and I put on a small amount of makeup. Mostly the usual: blush, mascara, and my favorite lip butter balm.

Wyatt's knock on the front door has me bending to

give Rudy one last scratch behind his ears on the plush living room floor, the sight of it bringing back vivid memories of the other night that have my face heating.

Now is not the time, Josie, I chastise myself and grab my small shoulder bag from the entryway table before opening the front door.

"Hi," Wyatt rasps, a sexy, lazy smirk lounging on his lips. His gaze travels the length of my body before he shakes his head. "You look beautiful, honey. So damn beautiful."

He's the one who looks... wow.

He traded in his old work jacket for a thick brown jacket, and beneath it, he's wearing a burgundy-colored henley with a pair of faded jeans that hug his muscular thighs. In his hands is a small bouquet of winter flowers that look like they've been cut directly from a garden.

When he sees me eyeing them, he chuckles, the sound slipping over me like a balm. "These are from Lucy and me. She insisted that we cut them out of Gram's garden."

The thought of the two of them doing that together is so adorable that it makes my chest ache.

"Thank you, Wyatt. That's so sweet and thoughtful," I murmur as I step forward and lift on my tiptoes to press my lips to his, earning me a low groan of approval as his tongue sweeps along the seam of my lips.

"Jesus, Josie, you taste so fucking good."

I laugh. "That's my lip balm. It's peppermint flavor."

"I guess peppermint just became my new favorite, then."

After I put the flowers in a vase with water on the kitchen table and give Rudy a very stern talking-to, warning him to stay away from them, Wyatt leads me to his truck with his hand clasped tightly in mine, then helps me into the passenger seat like a gentleman.

He slides in the driver's side, and then we're off. He still hasn't given me any clue as to where we're going, even though I try for most of the ride to get something, *anything* out of him.

Which drives me insane because he knows that I'm terrible with surprises.

But Wyatt just chuckles and places his big palm on my thigh, sweeping his thumb absentmindedly along the top.

I'm no less confused when he parks in front of the guest cabin that he and Lucy are calling home, then opens my truck door, offering me his hand with a teasing grin. "Let's go, beautiful."

Surprisingly, he doesn't lead me up to the porch. Instead, he leads me around the side of the house, and my brow furrows with confusion.

Okay, what is going on righ—

Oh my God.

I lift my hand to my mouth, covering it to stop the sound of shock from spilling past my lips.

We may be at Wyatt's house on his family's ranch, but this is *nothing* like the backyard I've seen before. It's been transformed into this beautiful, cozy… winter wonderland.

There have to be hundreds of lights strung up from posts to the porch, crisscrossing over the space that looks like something out of a movie.

There's a huge projection screen with the 1994 version of *Miracle on 34th Street* playing, because of course Wyatt would never forget that it's my favorite Christmas movie. In front of the projector is a small, cozy-looking couch that's covered in plush white blankets and snowflake-embroidered pillows. Situated between the couch and projector is a table that's been set for dinner with poinsettia china and a rich green and gold tablecloth, complete with red candlesticks that are flickering slightly from the wind. And there are a few fir trees lit up with sparkling twinkle lights framing the space.

He's thought of *everything*… even bringing the large outdoor heaters placed next to the couch to make sure we'd be warm despite the temperature.

I can't believe he did all of this. I was expecting maybe dinner and a movie. But this?

It's the most thoughtful, sweetest thing anyone has ever done for me.

Our own Christmas date night right in the middle of his backyard.

"But Lucy…" I trail off as I drag my gaze to his.

His mouth twitches. "At the main house with my grandparents for a movie night of her own."

He's taken care of it all.

"Wyatt…" I breathe, my throat suddenly feeling impossibly tight with emotion. I'm trying to find the right words, the right way to say thank you for putting this all together. "It's beautiful. I can't… I—"

He steps to me, sliding his arms around my waist and gently hauling me to him as he uses a finger to tip my chin up. "It's what you deserve, Josie. If I was even half the man I am today back then, I would've shown you that. I would've made sure you knew how important you were to me. Come on, let's go sit so we can talk."

I'm barely able to nod. I'm too overwhelmed by the emotions coursing through my body. My thoughts are a jumble of a hundred different things at once. Wyatt leads me to the couch and moves the thick, faux fur blanket so I can sit. I quickly shed my coat and then unzip my boots so I can draw my feet up in a crisscross as he takes the seat next to me, tossing the blanket over me and tucking the edges in.

It's such a sweet dad thing that it makes tears prickle behind my eyes. My emotions are going haywire.

"Wyatt, this is too much. It must've taken you all day to do this," I whisper thickly.

His shoulder dips while a broad grin curves his lips, and he reaches for my hand once more, threading his fingers through mine. "I had the best helper. Trust me, Lucy was so excited about our 'date' she could hardly sit still most of the day. I put her to work. It was actually her idea for the candles."

My gaze moves to the long, tapered candles in the middle of the place settings.

The sweetest touch that nearly makes my heart sing.

God, it's impossible not to feel everything for Lucy and Wyatt. How could I not? She's the sweetest angel, and Wyatt… well, he's him.

He's the same boy I've always known, but now, he's grown into a thoughtful, kind, compassionate man that I'm starting to fall for all over again.

Only now, there's so much more at stake. It's not only *my* heart or even his on the line; it's also Lucy's.

It's part of the reason that I'm so afraid to do this with Wyatt. Whatever *this* is. Because I don't want to be hurt again, but I can't stand the thought of Lucy being hurt by whatever happens between her father and me. Especially knowing what happened with her mother.

"I did all of this because I want to show you that I'm serious, Josie. I want another chance at having your heart. I want to make up for all the time that we lost, and this time, I want to do it right. I'm here, and I'm not going anywhere without you. Never again," Wyatt murmurs as his gaze burns into mine, sincerity flickering within the depths.

I truly don't believe that he'd ever purposefully hurt me.

But sometimes, love doesn't always happen the way you intended. We thought we were forever once before... but then, we weren't.

For a moment, I'm quiet as I try to find the right words. "I just need... some time. I want to be with you, right now, in *this* moment. But this is a lot, so fast, so please just give me some time, okay?" I finally say.

Without hesitation, he nods. "Whatever you need, Jos. I'm not going anywhere. For now, I'm just going to... woo you."

I toss my head back, laughing loudly. "Oh? Is that so?"

"Mhmmm," he hums, leaning forward and sliding his hand along the nape of my neck, pulling me gently to him. "I know how much Christmas does it for you, honey."

This handsome, thoughtful, crazy man. I sigh, reaching forward and tangling my fingers in the fabric of his shirt.

"Then by all means, Wyatt Owens, *woo* away."

He gives me an entirely too quick kiss and leaves me on the couch, disappearing through the back door of his house, only to return a few minutes later with a tray loaded down with food and a bottle of Strawberry Hollow's famous sweet red wine tucked beneath his arm.

"Ooooh, what is all this?"

"This," he says as he sets the tray on the table and starts arranging the dishes, "is your favorite from Patty's diner."

My eyes widen. "Chicken and dumplings?"

Wyatt nods. "And…."

He lifts the top off one of the platters, revealing my favorite dessert in the whole world. One that his grams makes, so one that I haven't had for many years.

"Pecan pie? Oh my God. You got Grams to make me this?" When he nods, I lean forward. "I have to skip dinner altogether and go straight for dessert."

"Whatever you want, honey." He laughs.

We eat completely out of order, starting with dessert, and then we have the main entree, and then back to the pecan pie because I can't get enough. Especially when Wyatt sucks the sweet filling off the tip of my finger, igniting a completely different type of hunger inside of me.

Once the plates are gone, I slowly crawl into his lap and straddle him, pulling the thick blanket tight around my shoulders as I stare down at him.

"Hmmm… what should we do now on our holidate?" I murmur, leaning closer. He grins against my mouth, and I press my lips gently to the corner of his and then another at the sharp edge of his jaw that's covered in his soft beard. The scrape against my lips is the most delicious feeling, and then my mind drifts back to the feeling in between my thighs. My core begins to tighten in response, a pulse of pleasure shooting through me as I recall it in vivid detail.

He palms my ass, squeezing and kneading the globes through my jeans. "I think it's time I have you for dessert, honey."

There's one thing that Wyatt's even better at than wooing... and that's devouring me, wholly and completely.

When he tightens his arms around me and stands from the couch, I yelp, inciting a low chuckle from him. He bends only to blow out the candles and then carries me up the back porch and through the back door, headed straight for his bedroom.

And now... I'm *curious*.

I've never been in his bedroom here before, and once he pushes the door open with his foot, carrying me inside and gently setting me onto the bed, I take it all in.

The large king-size four-poster bed, made with dark wood and a mattress that feels like it might actually be made of a cloud. The matching dresser and nightstand. It's masculine and modern yet somehow still gives an old feel to the craftsmanship.

"You look entirely too good in my bed, Josie," He

teases, the tone of his voice playful as he eyes me perched on the mattress.

My brow lifts. "Yeah?" I reach for the hem of my sweater and tug it over my head, tossing it to the floor. "What about... *now*?"

Wyatt prowls forward, a deliciously hungry look on his handsome face. "Now, you just look like *mine*, honey."

eleven

Josie Pearce is in my bed.

For eight long years, I never dreamed I'd get this opportunity again, and it hits me directly in the chest, nearly taking my fucking breath away. She might not be ready to admit it yet, but if there is anything I know with absolute certainty, it's that Josie is *mine*.

My fingers curve around her ankle as I gently tug her to the edge of the bed, drinking in the sweet sound of her giggle and mirroring her smile with a wolfish one of my own.

I'm going to devour her.

"I'm *starving*, honey. I think it's time for my favorite dessert," I rasp as I flick the button of her jeans open and waste no time dragging them down her full hips, letting them fall to the floor, leaving her in nothing but a matching set of red lace that makes my cock weep.

The lacy cup of her bra is cut low, offering me the smallest glimpse of her pink, rosy nipples.

As much as I love seeing her in this, I need it off her even more. I want to see her spread out on my bed, completely bare.

Lifting her foot to my shoulder, I dip my fingers into the waistband of her panties and tug them down, pressing kisses to the inside of her thighs, behind her knee, along her calf, her ankle.

Each press of my lips against her heated skin only makes me more desperate to taste her.

I toss the panties to the floor and move to work on her bra.

She shimmies out of the straps once I unclasp it, and finally, my eyes can slide over her bare flesh. Those pretty tits that fill my hands perfectly, the soft flare of her hips, her pretty, pink little pussy that's already wet and ripe for my tongue.

Instead of dropping to my knees in front of her, I reach behind my neck and pull my shirt off, then quickly get rid of my jeans and climb onto the bed beside her.

"Hold on here," I rasp as I settle on my back by the headboard. "And ride my face, honey."

I watch her eyes widen slightly, but she doesn't hesitate, crawling over to me and straddling my lower stomach. I can feel the wet, warm heat of her pussy along my abs, and the sensation has my cock twitching.

I grab fistfuls of her ass and drag her up until she's settled with her thighs on each side of my head, hovering above me.

Too fucking far.

My tongue darts out and swipes through her dripping pussy, gathering the taste of her on my tongue, a low, deep groan vibrating from my chest.

I fucking love the taste of her. I love eating her pussy. I could drown right here and die a happy man.

"Sit," I growl.

"God, you are so hot when you're all caveman-y, Wyatt," she says before lowering onto my mouth. I drag my tongue through her pussy, alternating between flicks to her clit and thrusting in her tight little hole until she's writhing above me, shamelessly chasing her orgasm.

I close my lips around her clit and suck, rolling it, alternating pressure.

Josie's hips rock on my face back and forth, over and over. She covers me until I can hardly fucking breathe, and I still want more.

"Good girl," I murmur against her slick pussy. "Come for me, honey, right now. Give it to me."

I love that my words only seem to spur her on. Her hips begin to move erratically, quick, shallow movements as her back bows and her climax rips through her. I can feel her thighs trembling as they bracket my ears, her breathless moans echoing around my bedroom.

"Fuck," I grunt, still lapping at her, wringing out all

of her pleasure with my tongue. I suck and lick until the aftershocks of her climax subside, and then I press one lingering kiss against her clit, chuckling when her hips buck.

"I don't think I'll ever recover from that," she says breathlessly, and I chuckle. She sits back on my chest, and in a split second, I have her beneath me, fitted between her thighs.

I flex my hips forward and press my hard, straining cock against her sensitive center, inciting a strangled breath from her lips. I capture it with my mouth as I sweep my tongue through her parted lips and flick her tongue with mine the same way I just ate her pussy. The tips of her toes slip beneath the waistband of my boxer briefs as she tries to push them down with her feet, not wanting to break our kiss, and I pull back, laughing.

"I've got it, honey."

Her dark eyes light up in amusement as she pulls her lip between her teeth and peers up at me and circles my cock with her fingers, pumping me. Her movements are as frantic as the buzzing beneath my skin, both of us desperate for the connection of the other.

Sometimes it feels like when we're together, we're making up for all of the time we've lost.

"Need to feel you on my cock," I grit out as I pull back, willing myself not to come before I've even gotten inside of her.

Smirking wickedly, she drags the head of my cock through her pussy, coating me with her arousal, then lining me up with her entrance. Without wasting a single fucking second, I thrust into her to the hilt, burying myself in her tight, wet heat until my eyes roll back.

A deep whimper tumbles out of my throat, a sound I'm not entirely proud of but a visceral response to having actual heaven wrapped around my cock that's making my vision dance.

This fucking woman might kill me.

"Fuuuuuck, Josie," I say, tossing my head back. I pull out of her until only the tip remains before slamming back inside. She lifts slightly and presses her lips to my throat, then rakes her teeth along my skin, which feels as if it's humming with a current. I'm losing my damn mind at how good she feels.

At having her in my bed for the first time as a man and not a teenager.

Kissing her.

Tasting her sweet little pussy.

Filling her with my cum until she's leaking down my cock.

I thrust into her over and over, fucking her so hard that her petite body is climbing the bed toward the headboard. The sound of our skin slapping together fills the room, the only sound aside from both of our harsh breathing and her soft moans as the head of my cock nudges against her cervix, pushing as deep as I can possibly go.

The caveman part of me hopes that my seed plants, that I can fill her belly with my baby. The thought alone almost has me losing the small amount of restraint I've managed to hold on to.

Josie pregnant with *my* baby.

Fuck. I can imagine it now, and I decide I like that thought way too goddamn much.

Before I can come, I pull out of her, panting so hard that my head swims.

"On your knees, honey."

She immediately complies, flipping onto her stomach as I rise to my knees behind her, palms curving around her hips and hauling her perfect, heart-shaped ass in the air.

Her cheek's pressed against the mattress as she waits to be fucked, and it's the sexiest thing I've ever experienced in my life.

Unable to help myself, I bend, lowering my mouth to her pussy and sliding my tongue through her, giving attention to her clit until her hips push back against my face.

I stand straight and once again grab her hip with one hand, and with the other, I feed my cock back inside of her, slamming home.

"*Oh my God,*" she cries out.

As I pound into her, my hips snap in rough, deep

strokes that have my balls tightening in desperation to empty inside of her. Arousal pools at the base of my spine, and I know I'm not going to last much longer.

It's impossible when she's squeezing my cock so tightly.

"I'm close," I warn, my voice a low grunt. "Need you to come with me, honey."

My eyes fall shut, and my head drops back against my shoulders as I fuck her, each thrust deeper than the last.

I reach around and use my thumb to strum her clit in quick, hard circles that have her tightening around me, that sweet little pussy starting to clamp down on me. "That's it. Are you going to come for me like a good girl?"

My girl loves to be praised, and I know it because the second I whisper those words, her entire body pulls taut, and she trembles as her orgasm courses through her.

She cries out my name, the best sound in the fucking world, and with one more deep thrust, I erupt inside of her, filling her with my cum in thick lashes until my balls are empty and my chest is heaving.

Josie collapses against the mattress, and I withdraw, my eyes zeroing in on the trail of cum that slips out of her, a surge of possessiveness moving through me.

I stand from the bed and move to the bathroom,

grabbing a washcloth from the cabinet and running it under hot water before padding back to my bedroom.

The corners of her lips rise sleepily where she's on her side.

"Let me take care of you, honey," I murmur as I open her thighs and drag the warm cloth between her legs.

Once I'm finished, I toss it into the hamper and lie down beside her, dragging her pliant body into my arms. I press my lips to the top of her head and drink in the feel of having her in my arms, sated and sleepy.

Part of me can't even believe that she's here right now, and the other part?

Knows I'm never going to let her go.

I'VE ALWAYS BEEN an early riser.

Most days, I'm up with the sun, out working on the ranch far before most of the town is even awake. There's always something to be done, and I prefer to get up early when it's quiet and still. But this morning... pulling myself out of bed was next to impossible with Josie's warm body draped over my chest, the morning sun starting to crest over the horizon and bathing her creamy skin in its warm morning rays.

I couldn't stop staring at the woman in my arms. The

The Christmas List

woman of my dreams. The woman I want to wake up with for all of the sleepy, quiet mornings I'll have in this house. Or another if that's what she wanted.

I'd build it with my bare fucking hands if that's what she needed from me. I'd give Josie Pearce anything. Including my last name, the second she'll let me.

I just have to give her time to get there. To let down her guard and give me the chance to prove to her that there's nothing I want more than this simple, beautiful life with her and Lucy.

California never felt like home to me. It was too big and loud and full of energy, even in the middle of the night. Deep down, buried beneath the exhaustion and hope of trying to give Lucy the best life I could, I knew that Strawberry Hollow was where we were meant to be.

So it's not surprising that we ended up here. In the place that would always be home.

In the place where I left a piece of my heart behind with Josie.

And now, I just want to make it my home again, with Josie and my daughter.

I could spend hours lying here and watching Josie sleep, drinking in every inch of her, desperate to commit all the little details to memory. The delicate slope of her nose and the constellation of freckles scattered along her cheeks, the slight upturn of her top lip. The tiny scar that mars her cheekbone from when she fell when we were kids, trying to climb the same tree her brothers and I did.

Most of my childhood memories include Josie, and I want her to be part of all my future ones too.

Carefully, I untangle myself from Josie and grab my boxer briefs from the floor, dragging them up my hips. With how late I kept her up last night, I don't want to wake her. Every time I thought we were done, one of us would reach for the other, and then suddenly, I would be inside her again. With my tongue, my fingers, my cock.

Her riding me, me taking her over the edge of the couch while those bright red nails bit into the couch cushions.

We were insatiable in a way I've never experienced.

It wasn't enough. I don't think it ever will be.

Padding quietly into the kitchen, I pull out everything I'll need for breakfast and get started. When my girl wakes up, I want to bring her breakfast in bed, and my one specialty?

Chocolate chip pancakes. Lucy bug's favorite, and knowing Josie and her sweet tooth, she'll love them too.

Just as I'm plating the last couple of pancakes, I get a text from Grams saying that Lucy is dying to come home to see "Miss Josie."

I set my phone on the counter and walk back to my bedroom, striding over to where Josie's still bundled beneath the covers. The large blanket has pulled low on her naked frame, exposing her back and the swell of her perfect ass.

Hell, everything about her is perfect.

Sitting on the edge of the bed, I tenderly ghost my fingers down her spine, then brush back a lock of her dark hair that's fallen over her cheek.

"Honey."

At first, she doesn't stir, so I lean down and press my mouth against the corner of her plush lips, trailing my kisses lower to the sensitive spot between her shoulder and neck.

She lets out a breathy sigh that has my cock twitching in my boxer briefs.

I could listen to those little sounds she makes for the rest of my life and never get tired of it.

"Wake up, honey."

Finally, she cracks open an eye, giving me those dark brown eyes I could drown in and a cute, sleepy smile.

"Good morning." Her voice is low and raspy from sleep.

I grin. "Morning, honey."

"Mmm. What time is it?'"

Leaning down, I cup her cheek and give her an unhurried kiss before pulling back. "Just after ten. I made you breakfast. And... Lucy wants to come say hi, but I wanted to check with you first."

"Of course. I always want to see Lucy." She smiles, and my heart squeezes in my chest.

I wish she truly knew how much it means to me that she has this easy, completely effortless relationship with my daughter.

Both of my girls together.

It's a dream.

As much as I would love to stay in bed with her all day, the second she learns that Lucy's going to be heading this way soon, she's up and dressed and at the kitchen table waiting for her within minutes.

Not long after, Luce comes bounding through the front door full of excitement and heads straight for Josie, colliding with her in a hug.

"Miss Josie! You're at my house."

Josie laughs, wrapping her arms around her, in no rush to let her go. "I am, sweetheart. And guess what? Your daddy made you your favorite." Lucy's eyes widen when she spots the stack of pancakes. "Chocolate chip."

"This is the best day ever!" Lucy claps as she drops her backpack to the floor and slides into the kitchen chair next to Josie.

I make them both a plate and join them at the table, mostly just observing both of them lost in conversation about Christmas with a wide smile on my face that I couldn't wipe away even if I tried.

Unable to deny that having Josie here with us feels like it's exactly where she belongs.

Josie

~~Hopelessly in love with Wyatt Pearce~~ **twelve**

"This is my *favorite* Christmas song! Even *more* than Rudolph the Reindeer! Definitely more than Frosty the Snowman! I love reindeer," Lucy says as she bounces around the living room, the jingle bells on her reindeer slippers ringing every time her foot hits the floor. Her cheeks are rosy pink from the warm glow of the fire and the fact that she hasn't taken a breath in at least an hour.

She's *slightly* cracked out on the amount of sugar in the three cups of her dad's hot cocoa she's had tonight.

It's been the most entertaining night watching Wyatt attempt to wrangle her in.

Unsuccessfully, of course.

Christmas is right around the corner, and she's got an endless tap of energy and excitement. Not just for the holiday but also because in a couple of days, they're going to announce the winning team of the Christmas List.

She and Wyatt turned our completed list in earlier today at Town Hall, and he said that she was so excited she was trembling when she handed in the paper. I love being able to experience her excitement outside of the classroom.

I love that I get to be a part of Lucy's life, in whatever capacity.

When he asked me over for dinner this evening, I was a little worried because we haven't really talked about how what's going on between us is going to affect Lucy. Or how we should act in front of her now that *something* more is happening between us. But I'm just trying to go with the flow and let Wyatt take the lead. He knows what's best for his daughter, and I trust that he'll make the right decisions when it comes to how to handle this with her.

"You know what I'm the most excited about, Miss Josie?" Lucy asks, flopping down on the floor in front of me and placing her chin in her hands.

"What?"

"Presents." Her bright green eyes flare with excitement. "I know that Christmas is about giving, not receiving, but it sure is fun to get presents. All of those are mine." She points to the pile of pink-wrapped presents under the tree.

My heart stutters when I think about Wyatt wrapping Barbie dolls and teacup sets in pink wrapping paper for his little girl.

Even if there are some uneven corners and I think maybe a small piece missing on the side of one gift, it's still the most adorable thing ever.

"Presents are *very* exciting. But it's good that you know that Christmas is about giving too. There's room for both." I grin, giving her a wink. I bring the glass of eggnog to my lips and take a small sip. I've been nursing the same glass since I got here, too distracted by Lucy to focus on much else. "Did you make your list for Santa already?"

She nods enthusiastically. "Yep. And I even made an *extra* copy. Grams dropped it in the mail for me!"

God, she's so adorable. One list to Santa isn't enough; there, of course, had to be two.

"One for backup, right?" I tease.

Lucy pops up from the floor, the bells of her slippers jingling loudly. "Yes. Daddy says you can never be too careful with the mail. That's why he made sure to bring our most important things, like the special ornaments, with us on the plane when we moved. So they wouldn't get lost." She points to their Christmas tree, and I can't help the smile that curves my lips.

I'm pretty sure if she had it her way, the tree would be pink. But Wyatt made true on his promise and gave her a tree of her own in her bedroom.

My gaze moves to the tree, admiring all of the little

touches it's apparent that she's added. A princess ornament, a butterfly—pink, of course, which I've now learned is her favorite color, even over purple—and a mermaid that glitters every time the light hits it.

There's even a sparkling star fitted on the top that I just know was a Lucy pick and not her dad's.

My perusal stops suddenly when my eyes catch on a familiar ornament tucked into the front branches, partially hidden from view, and my heart nearly stops in my chest.

Rising from the couch, I set the glass of eggnog on the side table and walk to the tree to peer closer, convinced that my eyes have to be playing tricks on me. Maybe I had more of the eggnog than I realized. Mrs. Scott's famous eggnog *is* known for being potent.

But... no. It's not the eggnog.

My hand is trembling as I lift it to the ornament, running my fingers over the smooth glass, a pang of nostalgia shooting to my heart.

Oh my God...

"What's wrong, Miss Josie?" Lucy asks.

When I glance down, the space between her brows is furrowed as she peers up at me. With my free hand, I swipe a tear that's fallen away.

"Oh, nothing, sweetheart. Do you know anything about this ornament? Is it... one of your daddy's special ones?"

Lucy nods. "Yes. We have had that one a looooong

time. It might be older than my papa. And he's like a... *dinosaur!*"

Her giggle is soft and sweet. "This is the only one I can't put on the tree because it's special to Daddy, and sometimes I accidentally drop things. I get to put the rest though!"

I know that she truly has no idea how special this ornament is.

Wyatt kept it.

All these years... he *kept* it. He could've thrown it away. I honestly thought he had. Why would he keep it when he made the decision to end things between us and leave me behind?

He kept the silly, inconsequential ornament that we made together, one for each of our trees, when we were teenagers during our first and only Christmas as a couple. Except it isn't at all inconsequential to me.

It means *everything*.

It means that even though he left, he couldn't let it go. He didn't let the memory of us go.

And I know because *I* still have the exact same ornament on my tree... because I couldn't let him go either.

My mind is spiraling in a hundred different directions at once.

"Alright, dessert is served, my ladies!" Wyatt calls from the dining room, causing me to drop my hold on the ornament. "Although, I am not sure *you* need any more sugar tonight, Lucy bug. You might not sleep till the New Year."

I hear Lucy giggle, and I imagine it's followed by an eye roll as she says, "Impossible, Daddy. Humans need at least eight hours of sleep a night. Miss Josie told me in class!"

I quickly swipe away another escaped tear and plaster on a bright smile as I make my way into the dining room. But I can't stop thinking about the ornament or the fact that he kept it.

"You think I'll ever get her to calm down tonight?" Wyatt whispers near my ear as I join him at the table.

I shake my head. "Probably not. But she's having fun, that's all that matters."

He chuckles. "You're right. But… I'm the one who's gotta handle bedtime." He pauses momentarily, his eyes searching mine as he reaches for my hand and sweeps his thumb lightly along my knuckles. "You're awfully quiet tonight, honey. Everything okay?"

"Yeah, of course." I smile. "I just can't believe that Christmas is almost here. It always passes so quickly. It feels like I have so many things to do."

I can't tell him what's truly on my mind right now because I'm still trying to… make sense of it.

I think I've just been so afraid of what happened in the past that I've been stuck there.

I keep thinking about everything that's happened between Wyatt and me all those years ago instead of letting myself truly see what's happening between us right now. I've been so scared about the possibility of getting hurt again that I haven't stopped to consider that neither of us are the same people that we were all those years ago.

Back then, we were… *kids.*

And we're not those same young, naïve kids anymore. *Eight years* have gone by, and I've been so stuck in the past that I haven't allowed myself the chance to look forward. To embrace all that we could be instead of being so fixated on what we were.

The realization is jolting… but also oddly freeing. Pulling myself out of my head, I settle myself into the dining table next to Wyatt, giving him a small smile.

Once Lucy's finished her dessert, a molten lava cake that she begged her dad to make for her, we move back to the couch, and she settles in between me and Wyatt.

His arm slips around her shoulder, and she sighs happily as she cuddles against his side and tangles her small fingers in his.

"Alright, bug, ready for your story?" Wyatt asks.

She nods. "Yes, please. Can we read the how to catch Rudolph one? I'm taking notes." Giggling, she taps her temple.

I can't even help but smile at how ridiculously adorable she is. I joked at first that she clearly had Wyatt wrapped around her finger, but now I think I'm wrapped around it too.

In the few weeks that I've known her, I've fallen hopelessly for this sweet, darling little girl.

And... now I'm not too scared to admit to myself that I've fallen for her father too.

I care about them so much that it outweighs the fear and uncertainty about the future. If I let those insecurities win? Then I wouldn't have Lucy or Wyatt in my life, and the thought of that makes my heart ache in the worst way.

In a way that I know will hurt infinitely more than if I took the chance and it somehow didn't work out between us.

Lucy and Wyatt... they're worth the risk.

Wyatt chuckles, searching through the stack of books she brought from her room until he finds the one she asked for. Lucy is all about her options, so of course, there are at least five here to choose from.

He opens it to the first page and starts reading, but he doesn't get very far because she wants to point out all of the things we were learning in class the last couple of weeks before Christmas break. She points to the author's and illustrator's names, then to the picture, and tells him that it's an illustration that can help explain the story, and then she excitedly swipes the book from his hand and closes it, pointing out the spine.

My chest swells with pride and emotion. She's so smart, and curious, and joyful.

I watch the two of them together as he begins to read

again, and she finally quiets long enough to immerse herself in the story. When her eyes slowly start to droop, Wyatt grins down at her, his face a mask of total adoration for his strawberry blonde beauty. The battle with sleep finally becoming a victor, her eyes flutter closed.

Wyatt peers down at her, swiping away a lock of hair from her face, and continues to read, only in a quieter voice. Because even though she's asleep now, he promised he would read the entire book, and he doesn't want to break a promise to his daughter. The moment is so simple and innocent, but it's a testament to what an incredible father he is. What an amazing *man* he is. She would never know the difference, but it matters to him.

My heart squeezes tightly in my chest as emotion claws its way up my throat, and I realize that I am deeply and hopelessly in love with Wyatt Owens. Every version of him.

I never stopped loving him, and now I love Lucy just as much.

And I might not know what the future holds, unable to predict if I'll end up hurt in the end... again. But what I do know is that Wyatt will hold my heart with care, respect, and pride the same way he holds his daughter's.

And that's enough for me.

They're enough for me.

~~Christmas List Winners~~ **thirteen**

"Daddy, are you paying attention? They're about to tell us who won!" Lucy cries, tugging on my hand.

Honestly? I wasn't paying much attention to the stage because I was staring at Josie, unable to pull my eyes away from her. She's standing beside me, laughing at the story that Grams is telling her about Lucy, her pretty red-painted lips curved in a broad smile that takes my breath away.

I don't think I'll ever stop being taken by surprise by how beautiful she is. How perfectly she fits with Lucy and me. How right it feels to have her standing next to me as if we're already a family.

Something I can only dream about happening.

"Yeah, bug." I smirk, peering down at Luce. "I'm paying attention. But you know, even if we don't win, you still get to meet Santa, right?"

She nods, giving me a slight huff. "Yes, but I want to ride with him on the float and throw candy."

Of course she does, and I want her to be able to too, but even if we didn't win the competition today, I think I still won.

Because I've got her and Josie.

I nod as I reach for Lucy's hand, threading my fingers in hers, squeezing reassuringly.

"Is she nervous?" Josie whispers near my ear, and I nod, turning to look at her. Worry mars the space between her brows, furrowing it deeply, and I chuckle.

"She's fine. She's a lot like you in the way that she's competitive as hell. She wants to ride with Santa."

"I hope we win," Josie finally says, reaching for my other hand, slightly surprising me. I know she's been... more hesitant about things with us, despite the incredible sex we've had and how amazing the last few weeks have been.

I understand her feelings, and I wasn't lying when I said that I would wait for however long she needed. I'm in this for the long haul, and I intend to prove that to her.

Not just for me but for Lucy too.

Last night, when I was putting her to sleep, tucked beneath her pink mermaid covers, she looked at me and asked, "Daddy, are you less grumpy because Miss Josie loves you?"

I almost swallowed my damn tongue.

"What do you mean?" I'd asked.

She chewed the corner of her lip, pushing her hair out of her face. "It's just... one time Miss Josie said that when people are grumpy, sometimes they just need extra love. I think you're not so grumpy now because you have my love *and* Miss Josie's. Right?"

There's no question that I love Josie. I've *always* loved Josie.

I loved her as a kid, and I love her now as a man.

And... it's important to me that Lucy's okay with that. Because she will always come first. She will always be the most important thing in my life.

So for a moment, I hesitated, mulling over the right response in my head before I finally said, "Would you be okay if Miss Josie loved me? And if I loved Miss Josie too?"

There wasn't a single second of hesitation in my daughter's face as her eyes lit up, and she nodded, a wide, toothless, yet very sleepy smile splitting her face. "Yes! *I* love Miss Josie sooo much, so I think you should too, Daddy."

Her little eyes fluttered shut a few minutes later, and she drifted off to sleep.

So, she didn't hear me as I whispered, "I already do, bug."

It was a pivotal moment, even though I know my five-year-old didn't realize how important it was, but having her blessing means everything to me.

The sound of Mayor Davis tapping on the microphone as he walks onto the stage pulls me from the memory of last night. I feel Lucy's fingers tighten in mine, and I laugh.

This girl.

Mayor Davis's pudgy cheeks are rosy as he walks further onto the stage. Today's outfit is no less festive than all the rest have been. He's got on a full three-piece suit in bright red velvet, paired with a green top hat with a plaid ribbon. Truly never fails to surprise me.

"Good afternoon, everyone! Today is finally the day. I know you have all been working very hard to complete this year's list, and I am excited and proud to announce the winner of our annual Christmas List competition!"

A sea of applause sounds around the packed town square as the crowd's excitement ramps up. It seems like everyone in town participated this year. I guess Mayor Davis was right. Even though I originally wasn't interested at all in doing the competition or any of the festive shit at first, the competition really did get everyone involved and in the Christmas spirit. It definitely has made this Christmas one to remember.

Though, for me, it's not only the list that's responsible for that.

"I just want to say thank you to everyone for participating and for really working so hard to bring the entire town of Strawberry Hollow together to celebrate the season. After all, it's the entire reason we have this competition in the first place." He smiles and reaches into his coat pocket and pulls out a gold envelope, raising it above his head and twirling it through his fingers. "Now, without further ado, this year's winners are…"

There's a dramatic pause, one that nearly electrifies the crowd, including my daughter, who's bouncing around on the tips of her toes. "Team Rowdy Reindeers! Congratulations! You will be riding with Santa in today's parade!"

My jaw falls open as he announces our team. Lucy screams, jumping up and down with the biggest smile I think I've ever seen her wear, and she runs to Josie, who joins in the cheering and jumping.

God, I love these girls.

These Christmas-obsessed girls of mine.

"Daddy!" Lucy exclaims. "We won! Can you *believe* it!"

I laugh, shaking my head. "I can't, bug. Go on, go up there and meet Santa."

The crowd around us is cheering and clapping, and that only seems to make Lucy more excited. She doesn't have to be told twice. She drops Josie's hands, turning and sprinting for the stage.

I can feel Josie step back beside me, her hand slipping in mine, and when I glance down at her, those beautiful brown eyes are full of unshed tears.

"What's wrong, honey?" I say, turning to slip my hands around the edge of her jaw, cradling her in my palms.

"I'm just... I'm happy, Wyatt. I'm so happy that it feels like my heart might actually burst," she whispers quietly, so quietly that I can barely hear her over the buzz of the crowd.

"If you're happy, then I'm happy, Josie girl."

I watch as the column of her throat moves as she swallows, giving me a sweet smile. "I need to say something, Wyatt."

"What's going on?" My brow lifts, a sliver of anxiousness coursing through me.

Fuck, I hope I haven't pushed her too ha—

"I love you, Wyatt Owens. I have loved you since I was ten years old. Even when you weren't here, a part of me loved you."

Holy shit.

I'm still trying to let her words, the words I've been desperate to hear, sink in when she continues, those unshed tears now freely falling and wetting her cheeks. "It just... took a little while for my head to catch up with my heart. My heart seems to have always known that we'd somehow find our way back to each other. Even when I was too afraid to admit it." She blows out a shaky breath and then sucks in an inhale as if trying to collect herself. "Wyatt, I've been living in the hurt of our past, and that's not fair to either of us."

"Josie..." I start, but she shakes her head in my hands, and I sweep a fresh tear away.

"Let me finish, please. I can't wait another moment to tell you this," she whispers, peering up at me through tear-soaked lashes, continuing when I nod. "I'm scared. Terrified, really. But last night, spending time with you and Lucy at home, doing nothing... I realized how much doing nothing with you means to me. How every moment I spend with both of you, I never stop smiling. My heart never stops squeezing at all of these little moments that, before you, I never considered to be special but that are now so incredibly special to me." Josie pauses, laughing on a watery sob. "I realized that there's nowhere else I would rather be than with you. *Both* of you. There's no one else that I could imagine spending my Christmas with. There's no one else that I would rather do a Christmas competition with and jump into freezing water that stole my breath. You steal my breath *every* single day, Wyatt Owens."

Her dark eyes hold mine, burning into me, searing their way into my heart in a way that I know will never fade.

I can't believe she's saying that she feels the way I do.

Fuck, how often have I wished for this very moment in the last few weeks? Willing her to take my hand and jump with me.

"So what I'm saying is that I love you, I love your

daughter, and I don't need time or to think about that. I want to be with you, and I trust that you'll protect my hear—"

I lower my mouth to hers before she can even finish, cutting her off with a kiss that I feel in the depths of my damn soul, and I know that she does, too, by the way her hands fist in the front of my shirt and she sighs against my lips. I can feel it in the way she touches me, the way she kisses me back.

Josie may have been afraid to say it out loud or to even admit to herself what was happening between us, but I knew. From the moment I saw her again, I knew. I just needed to give her a second to get to where I was, and when she finally did?

It would feel just like this.

Like she was made for me, every inch of her, heart and soul.

I pull back and stare down at her, wearing a lovesick smile because I can't help it, even if I tried.

"Finally, you caught up with me, honey." I chuckle when her lip tilts. "I was waiting for you. I would've waited forever if that's what it took, Josie. I love you, and I'm not ever going to let another day go by where I don't show you that."

Her arms wind around my neck as she lifts on her toes and presses her lips to mine again. Red lipstick be damned, I'm going to kiss Josie Pearce wherever and whenever I want.

"We've got a lot of time to make up for, honey."

"We do. Good thing we make such a good team, then, huh?" she replies.

"The *best* team. It's me, you, and Luce forever, Josie. All I need is my girls, and I'll be the happiest man in the world," I whisper against her lips, dropping my forehead against hers.

"You've got us, Wyatt Owens. Always."

Standing in the middle of Town Square, my daughter on the stage laughing gleefully as she holds Santa's hand and the woman of my dreams in my arms, the only thing I can help but think is...

The only Christmas wish I've ever made has finally come true.

THE END

Josie

epilogue

**Christmas Eve
One Year Later**

I thought I couldn't possibly love Christmas as much as I already did. Being proverbially crowned Strawberry Hollow's Queen of Christmas was a title I rightfully earned with my overwhelming amount of festive spirit every year.

But then... Wyatt and Lucy walked back into my life and somehow made it even *more* special. More *memorable*. More *meaningful*.

And this year just might be the most special of them all.

"Lucy! Wyatt!" I call from the living room. "Can you come in here for a second?"

They've been working on a Christmas puzzle, one of

our new favorite traditions, for the last hour or so, which gave me just enough time to get my surprise ready.

Wyatt strides into the living room with Luce right on his heels, and I can't keep the smile from tilting on my lips.

God, this man is beautiful. He steals my breath on the daily, but seeing him wearing matching plaid Christmas pajamas with his daughter without a single complaint makes him the hottest husband in the world.

It still feels like a dream that I get to call Wyatt Owens my *husband*.

Our winter ceremony was small but had everyone we loved there with us. Even his papa was able to come now that his hip is fully healed.

We got married under the same tree that I fell from when we were kids, where he held me as I cried, and somehow, even then, I knew that I would someday be his.

It was magical, and even almost a month later, I'm still replaying our wedding day in my mind on repeat.

"Hi, honey," he rasps, pressing a sweet kiss to my lips as he sits beside me on the couch, the cushions dipping with his weight.

Lucy climbs into her daddy's lap, her bright green eyes fixing curiously on the two newly wrapped presents in my lap. "What's that, Mommy?"

My heart squeezes in my chest. I also can't believe that I get to be this little girl's *mama*.

She asked me a few months ago if she could call me Mommy, and I broke down in sobs right in the middle of the kitchen floor. My sweet girl thought she had done something wrong, and I had to quickly explain to her that it's an honor for her to call me Mommy, and there was nothing I would love more.

An honor that I hold so close to my heart.

My husband and my daughter are the light of my life. They're everything to me, bringing me more joy and happiness than I ever knew was possible.

Smiling, I lift the presents. "These... are very special presents that I have for you."

Wyatt looks completely confused because we already picked out all of Lucy's presents together, so this one we haven't discussed yet.

"Do you want to open them?"

Lucy nods enthusiastically as her eyes widen.

I hand her the pink-wrapped present that's tied with a pale purple bow and then hand Wyatt the burgundy box with the green bow.

"Can I open it right now?" Lucy asks, gaze flicking from her dad and me to the present and back, wearing a wide grin. I miss her toothless smile that I loved so much, but time continues to tick by, and my little girl is growing more and more every day.

The most bittersweet feeling, watching her grow right before my eyes.

I nod.

They both begin to open the presents. Lucy's strawberry blonde eyebrows are furrowed in deep concentration as she tries to get the bow off.

Wyatt manages to pull the paper off faster, so he grabs the small box from within and carefully pulls the lid off. At first, I see the confusion shadowing his face when he pulls out the small white ornament that's tied with a white satin bow along the top.

His eyes find mine after he reads the word written in gold script, and as badly as I tried to resist, I can't keep the tears from welling.

"What?"

I nod, a small sob bursting past my lips. "Yeah."

Lucy finally opens her box and pulls out the matching ornament. "B-i-g... S-i-s-t-e-r?" It takes a moment for her eyes to find me as she rereads the words a few times. "But... I'm not a sister."

I laugh. "Yeah, Lucy bug, you're going to be a big sister."

Her eyes widen as she shoots up from Wyatt's lap, almost dropping the ornament. "Really? I'm... I'm going to be a big sister? Is the stork bringing it?"

My gaze finds Wyatt's, and when I see the tears in his eyes, his handsome face full of so much love and surprise, I completely lose the battle of keeping the tears back.

"There's a baby in here, Lucy bug." I put my hand along my stomach, which will soon grow as our baby does, an overwhelming wave of emotion settling in my throat.

"Honey..." Wyatt murmurs. "We're having a baby?"

"We are. I'm eight weeks."

I can barely get the words out before his big, strong arms are circling me and hauling me off the couch into his arms. He buries his face in my neck, and I can feel his tears wetting my skin. "I love you, Josie. This is the most beautiful gift you could ever give me, honey. Thank you."

A powerful feeling swells in my chest as I curve my palm around his nape, holding him to me.

I'm making Wyatt a daddy again and Lucy a big sister, and the feeling is... indescribable.

I get to share something so special with the man I love with every piece of me. To build a family with him, a home that's bursting with love and happiness, memories that will never fade no matter how much time has passed.

I love this little life.

And most of all... I'm hopelessly in love with Wyatt Owens.

Want to read about Josie's older brother Jackson Pearce and his enemies to lovers romance with his Emma Worthington?

Turn the page for an *exclusive* sneak peek at chapter one!

festive feud sneak peek

Emma

I love Christmas *almost* as much as I loathe Jackson Pearce.

That's saying a lot since Christmas is *magical*.

There's just something... whimsical about the snow falling, lights twinkling along the Christmas tree, the smell of pine and fir fresh in the air. Traditions and family. The excitement you feel when you wake up on Christmas morning and rush to the tree. The sense of innocence and wonder that you hold on to well past your childhood years.

Yet somehow, Jackson Pearce *still* manages to ruin all of that.

"Emmie," he says, an arrogant smirk tugging at the corner of his full lips. One that I immediately want to wipe right off his stupidly handsome face.

Even *I* can't deny that the man is unfairly attractive. Even if I want to hit him with my car.

He's tall, at least over six foot three if I had to guess, with deep chestnut-colored hair and stubble to match. High cheekbones, warm whiskey eyes, a strong, sharp jaw. He's always been handsome, and truthfully, it only makes me detest him more.

How dare he be so attractive and yet the most annoying man to ever walk the planet.

And how absolutely rude of fate and the universe to put us together in Strawberry Hollow, which at times feels like the tiniest small town in America.

"It's *Emma*," I respond through clenched teeth. "I *hate* that you call me that."

"I know." He chuckles, plucking a stuffed Santa off the shelf and twirling it in his hand. I try not to watch the thick muscles of his forearms ripple as he does. He's got the whole "roll up the sleeves of my flannel to show off my hot, veiny forearms" thing down to a science. "Why do you think I do it?"

Rolling my eyes, I step away, ready to rid myself of this conversation and *him* as soon as possible.

All I wanted was to come to the general store today to pick up the limited edition nutcracker that I have been so patiently—okay, fine, *not* so patiently—waiting to arrive, and because apparently I've been on the naughty list, I've run into Jackson in the process.

It's not just that he does whatever he possibly can to push my buttons, or the fact that his ego is the size of

Town Square, or even that he calls me Emmie just to make my blood boil that makes me absolutely loathe him.

Sure, all of those things add to the already burning fire.

But the real reason that Jackson Pearce and I hate each other has everything to do with the fact that our families have been enemies for decades.

The Pearces vs the Worthingtons.

Our long-standing feud has gone back for over thirty years, starting when our parents first met.

The small-town version of the Capulets and the Montagues.

The Hatfields and the McCoys.

Jack Frost and Santa Claus.

The Grinch and the Who.

A rivalry that has withstood time and, at some points, rational thinking.

So even if he wasn't enemy number one for all of those reasons I listed, we were born to hate each other.

He just simply makes it easier to do so.

"What brings you out of the mansion, Emmie?" He invades my space once more, and I get a whiff of whatever cologne he's wearing. Bergamot and warm amber. Spice.

He smells delicious.

Add that to the list of things I hate about him.

"It's none of your bus—"

"Oh, she's here about the new nutcracker! Goodness, you know, I can't keep those things in stock. It's a shame—the manufacturer says it's the last restock of the season." Sweet, dear old Clara gestures to the lone nutcracker on the shelf, and my eyes widen.

No. No. No. *No.* Please, no.

This cannot be happening.

My eyes flit back to Jackson, whose brow is raised in question. For a moment, neither of us moves.

We engage in a silent stare-off.

His eyes dart from mine to the decoration and back, and it's as if I can read his thoughts.

I know exactly where this is going, which is why I'm the first to move, launching myself at the shelf so I can grab it first.

Except, of course, it doesn't work that way. Why would *anything* be easy when he's involved?

Both of us grab on to the nutcracker at the same time, our gazes locked on each other as we each hold on with no plans to let go.

"Put it down, *Pearce*," I whisper-yell as I yank it toward me.

He tugs it back toward him, pulling me along with it. "In your dreams, *Emmie*."

Yank. "God, you are the most annoying man I've ever met. Like you actually care about this damn nutcracker. You clearly only want it because *I* want it."

"No, I want it because it would be perfect for our Christmas party. You know not everything is about *you*, right?"

Tug.

Scoffing, I pull harder, yanking it back toward me in this ridiculous game of tug-of-war that we're engaging in. "Oh, that's fresh, coming from *you*. I'm surprised that your ego can even fit inside this building."

"Funny, because your 'too good for everyone' attitude makes it feel a *bit* stuffy in here," he retorts.

Tug.

Pull.

Yank.

"This is childish. Let go, Emmie. Be the bigger person."

"Never, Pearce."

This time, I yank harder than I have yet and lose my footing as I bump into the display behind me. I can feel the air in the room shift before it even happens.

The entire store has gone deathly quiet, and seconds later, there's the telltale clink of glass as the entire display behind me falls backward and plummets to the floor in a deafening shatter.

Oh. My. God.

A few seconds pass where I'm too afraid to move, like if I do, then I might further the already catastrophic damage that has ensued. Exhaling, I drop the nutcracker as if it's on fire, my eyes widened in shock as I slowly turn toward the ruins.

Glass ornaments are scattered along the floor in a heap of broken shards.

There are so many of them you can hardly see the floor beneath it.

My eyes dart to Clara's, her jaw agape in shock and a worrisome dip between her brows, her hand clutched to her chest like she needs to hold on to her heart. Slowly, her hand moves toward the ancient turn-dial phone next to her, and she lifts the receiver, dialing three numbers.

That's when I realize just how screwed we are, and it's *all* because of Jackson Pearce.

"WAYNE, come on. You've known me since I was in *diapers*. This feels a little extreme for just a minor… little disagreement," I mutter.

Wayne scoffs, shaking his head as he adjusts his hat lower, his shiny sheriff's badge glinting beneath the light of the general store. "Minor, Emma? You two"—he points between Jackson and me—"destroyed over ten thousand dollars' worth of merchandise! Let's not even get into the mess that poor Clara is going to have to deal with since the two of you are spending the night in lockup. You almost gave that sweet old lady a heart attack."

My jaw drops.

Lockup? As in... *jail*?

Not that Strawberry Hollow has an actual jail. It's more of just a small four-by-four cell with an old rusty door.

But still...

Surely he's not actually going to put me in a cell like some kind of... *criminal*. Wait until my parents hear about this. They might literally kill me.

"You're throwing us in the drunk tank? We're not even drunk, Wayne!" Jackson groans. "Come on, man. For once in my life, I have to agree with Emmie. We got into a small disagreement, and accidents happen. You know that. We'll pay for the damages and get everything cleaned up."

"Sure, I do." Wayne nods, crossing his arms over his chest. "But this was no dang accident, Jackson. Look, we've all had enough."

He pinches the bridge of his nose, exhaling as his eyes fall shut. When he opens them, they're filled to the brim with frustration. "Both of your families have been at this for years, and everyone in the town has had about enough of it. I mean it. You've given me no other choice."

I can see Jackson shake his head beside me before he retorts, "Yeah? This is going to make for a great conversation at the next poker night. Share a beer and tell all the guys about how you threw me in jail for fighting with Emmie Worthington."

I snort.

Of course, Jackson Pearce would play poker with the sheriff. Too bad that little detail isn't helping in this situation since we're about to spend the night in jail all because he's got the maturity level of a teenage boy.

Some of us have grown up, but he's obviously still the same immature boy from when we were in school.

Clearly, this is all of his fault.

If he would've just let go of the stupid nutcracker and left me the hell alone, then none of this would have happened in the first place.

But no, he had to go and try and one-up me, as he and his family *always* have done.

"Yeah, well, maybe both of you shouldn't have gotten into a fight in the middle of the general store and broken a whole bunch of shit, then, huh? Now, let's go. Don't make me handcuff you."

My eyes widen as panic rises in my throat. "You… wouldn't."

His brows rise. "Try me."

Great.

Add felon to the list of my most attractive qualities.

Click HERE to continue reading!

A Festive Feud is currently available to read for **_FREE_** in Kindle Unlimited.

Start the series with **Book One** of the Strawberry Hollow series, The Mistletoe Bet which features Quinn Scott.
Click HERE to read for free.

need moore?

Want to purchase signed copies, exclusive editions, merch and more? Click HERE to go to my book store.

Want instant access to bonus scenes, exclusive giveaways, and content you can't find ANYWHERE else?

Sign up for my newsletter here and get all of the goods!

In your audiobook era? Find all of my audiobooks here!

Want to chat with me about life, get exclusive giveaways and see behind the scenes content? Join my reader group Give Me Moore

also by maren moore

Totally Pucked

Change on the Fly

Sincerely, The Puck Bunny

The Scorecard

The Final Score

The Penalty Shot

Playboy Playmaker

Orleans U

Homerun Proposal

Catching Feelings

Walkoff Wedding

Standalone

The Enemy Trap

The Newspaper Nanny

Strawberry Hollow

The Mistletoe Bet

A Festive Feud

The Christmas List

about the author

Maren Moore is an Amazon Top 20 Best-selling sports romance author. Her books are packed full of heat and all the feels that will always come with a happily ever after. She resides near the bayou in Louisiana with her husband, two little boys and their fur babies. When she isn't on a deadline, she's probably reading yet another Dramione fan fic, rewatching cult classic horror movies, or daydreaming about the 90's.

You can connect with her on social media or find information on her books here ➡ here.

www.ingramcontent.com/pod-product-compliance
Lightning Source LLC
LaVergne TN
LVHW041803060526
838201LV00046B/1103